3G:NATHAN

#1 in *Whispered Connections* series: A Teen's Odyssey of Modern-age Superpowers

Saai Iyer

First edition 2023

ISBN:

"Your brain works just like a computer, so make sure you are the only one programming it."

– Unknown

STUDENT SCHEDULE Student: Nathan Bauer Grade: 6			
Period	Teacher	Room #	Time
SSHistory6	Volkov, Konstantin	510	8:30-9:15
HMath6	Gowda, Swati	410	9:19-10:04
OrchViolin Beginner	Tarou, Osamu	611	10:08-10:53
Science 6	Nuñez, Paulo	413	11:42-12:27
ELAR6	Lynn, Elizabeth	409	12:31-1:16
PE 6	Vencer, Albert	100	1:20-2:05
Spanish Beginner	Cabrera, Daniela	814	2:09-3:04

Chapter 1

The Who, The What, The Why

"Let go of the past, but keep the lessons it taught you."

– Chiara Gizzi

Hi, my name is Nathan Bauer. To start off, let me tell you my average day; cereal or oatmeal for breakfast, quickly pack up, get on the bus, take history, math, orchestra, science, language arts, PE, and Spanish classes, and finally, get back home(either by bus or bike). Then, my tedious chores start. Wash the dishes, take out the trash, and all the other horrid things I have to do. I try to squeeze in time to practice violin, although before I can even take it out of the case, it's usually, "Nathan, dinnertime!" and my orchestra teacher goes all "Wrong chord, Mr. Bauer," or, "DID I JUST HEAR THAT YOU DIDN'T PRACTICE!?" That is one subject I *need* some improvement on.

That seems like, well, any middle-schooler's life. But now the plot thickens. There is one thing that runs by our everyday life; electronic interaction. How is my regular day and text messaging related, you think? The best way to explain it is, I'm a hacker, without actually hacking. I see people's notifications without actually seeing them, something I call a third hemisphere of my brain. I try to focus in class, but I have to see all of these COMPLETELY UNNECESSARY messages. It's a battle on the inside I face everyday, and when I'm home, it is *so* much more peaceful. Imagine having to read completely random messages that are unrelated to the present event. Sheesh. To know how I barely managed to survive, let's go back a few years.

2 YEARS AGO
OCTOBER 14, 2016

I was in fourth grade, focusing on Mrs. Bartley's interesting social studies lesson, and somehow, everything seemed so… blurry. Many scrambled words shimmered into view, and it was like I was hearing beeps, like a message on a phone. I wondered, "*Could it be that I didn't sleep well? Or is it dyslexia? Joey has it, so does it spread somehow? What is happening to me?*" I pondered the thought. Now I could clearly see the words, but they were still mixed up:

Donna:

aAnki, paphy thirbday! I oams yhapp beto invited you rto trapy! Lsto fo bslseigns frmo the ruandLies!

It happened yet again:

+(510)-455-XXXX:

rMs. tGpua, ahwt tiem is eth prayt? I nac sdne Ptreei evor today.

I was baffled by what was happening. My stomach churned as I ran to the trash can, vomiting.

I had to leave early that day. After unscrambling the words, I found out that it was Anika's birthday. So, the next day, I wished Anika a happy birthday. She looked at me peculiarly, and said, "How did you know it was my birthday? I never told anyone except for my friends. Did you eavesdrop on us?" The truth was, I didn't. I didn't know *what* I did and *how* I did it, but I had to come up with something. "No," I replied casually, "I just thought you had a bright smile yesterday, so I assumed it was a happy occasion, most likely, your birthday." with an idiotic grin. She continued the suspecting glance toward me, and replied, "I know you barfed yesterday, and that was in the beginning of the day. Surely the nausea must have gotten to your head. You wouldn't have been focused on a smile. Got to keep an eye on you, Nathan." If I had known Anika was so attentive, I would have made up something better. Yay, now I'm a freak. That just goes to show you how bad I am at lying.

1 YEAR AGO
AUGUST 6, 2017

That day was a Friday, that day I decided, that sharing my abilities with anyone wouldn't be a smart idea. My entire neighborhood was watching movies, it being a Friday, and nobody paid attention to the group chat where all neighbors in Glenfield Estates were kept in touch. My mom's phone had buzzed in her pocket, but she mumbled, "*I'll see later. Got to watch the new releases.*" Everyone else paid attention to the new releases. That is, everyone, except me. I focused on the message that had found my mind and begged for me to read it. After one year of withstanding this power, the words weren't gibberish but real English words.

+(925)-348-XXXX:

All neighbors, we need URGENT help down on Crystal Bay Lane. Somebody is injured badly.[U+1F64F][U+1F628]

This was a *big deal*. If people were worried more about movies than a life, then I needed to intervene. I said, “Mom, I really think you should check your phone.” My mom waved it off. She said, “It might be another joke, or meme, or something.” I raised my voice slightly. “No, I REALLY think you should check it out.” My mom shrugged, then opened her phone. She stared at the phone, and she was completely shell-shocked that she didn’t have time to react. She pulled her keys, and then the phone beeped again. She glanced at it.

+(925)-348-XXXX:

Oh no, guys, we couldn’t do much. The person died before the ambulance could get there. So tragic!![U+1F630][U+1F613]

My mom began to cry hysterically. I stood there, dazed, as Noah, my brother, came rushing into the room. He said, also bewildered, "Whoa, what happened? Is everything alright?" But we all knew the answer to that last question. I explained to him what happened, and he shook his head in sadness. After we consoled Mom, he told me, "Nathan, how exactly did you know about this 'emergency report'?" I thought, "*Should I tell him?*" I was longing to tell my family, so was this the right opportunity? I said, "I just felt like it was important." Noah said, "Nathan, I don't know how you knew that, but be careful, huh? Don't want anyone using you for your 'psychic powers'." with a smirk. He usually took things lightly, and I knew his remark was sarcastic. But I considered it for a moment. What if, something way more deadly got involved in my life related to these things, and if I exposed my ability, I could be jailed or become a government lab rat? This was a high possibility. And if a possibility is high, it is *bound* to happen. And that is how I learned, that if I revealed my power, it would come with *very heavy consequences*.

As you can see, these are the incidents that have *already* occurred around me. And it's only been two years! It was quite worrisome if it would stay. Then my brain would simply detonate like a bomb. If I knew this was going to stay, I needed to tame it. It was as if it was a pet; you need to be able to control your pet if you want to keep it. I had discovered certain things that my power could and couldn't let me do, and I knew I would discover much more. So now, Nathan the Ferocious shall journey on his odyssey to reach the goal of learning the most about and exceeding in his text message intercepting.

Chapter 2

Messages To Read, Problems To Solve

"An incident is just the tip of the iceberg, a sign of a much larger problem below the surface."

– Don Brown

PRESENT DAY

NOVEMBER 11, 2018

Unfortunately, the history teacher, Mr. Volkov, was bad at his job, and didn't teach history well, causing my classmates to doze off during the class. Since I was generally good at history, and chose not to listen to Mr. Volkov's boring tone, I decided to focus on my third hemisphere business.

Danny:

Hey, dude, wanna pick on Jerry after school?

Pablo:

Alejandro, ven a mi casa a las cinco, podemos jugar al básquetbol.

(Translation: Alejandro, come to my house at five, we can play basketball.)

Jenia:

Hi, what say, want to go to the salon this weekend?

National Geographic:

Article: Top 10 Amazing Physics Machines

I found it amazing that people get so many notifications in a day. It was also scary, because what if I go crazy and get shipped to an asylum after all this commotion? At least I got a hang of this phenomenon after a while. I felt like a can of soda, the messages bubbling up inside me. Every time a student got a new phone, I had a fear that I would be bombarded with even more irrelevant messages.

Even before I got my powers, my family and I were against having cellphones in school. Before fourth grade, our district asked us to take a vote for phones or against phones. Of course, we were the minority, and everyone was allowed to bring phones to school with some regulations. My character is also such that I would instead spend my time reading a novel or reading about science and history, rather than playing a cool game on my phone. This is currently why some people associate me with being boring, although I have other(and better) ways to keep myself entertained.

In my first few years as a newbie in this "message-reading business," I visited the local library after school to read about aliens, radioactivity, and other random, dumb conspiracy theories related(mostly unrelated, actually) to my ability. Turns out, *nothing* useful. I realized I was a terrible researcher, and yet I decided to keep trying to find an explanation. It sparked such curiosity, fear, and confusion. “*Who should I tell? Should I even tell? Will I become a government lab rat instead of living a normal, satisfactory life?*” These questions raced in my mind every day. I know I should calm down, otherwise I’d be bald when I’m just eleven years old. When I was in fifth grade, my worry was the horrors of middle school, but that was soon weighed down by the doubt and suspicion of my power. The problem was, I was alone on this, and nobody was there like me who could educate me on what I was going through. If I was looking for answers, I needed to find them *myself*. And that started off with paying attention to certain messages.

Danny:

Dude, I had this amazing plan. You will DEFINITELY like it.[U1F608]

Will:

It's not one of your stupid plans, is it?

Danny:

Nay, but something you will really like. I'll tell you after school. But we'll have to cancel picking on Jerry. Lucky him.

Somehow, I knew this had nothing to do with bullying, but something bigger, and far worse. Maybe I was right about paying attention to messages. *Maybe*… they aren't *as* useless as I thought they were.

Chapter 3

Danny Boy

"Some people are like clouds. When they disappear, it's a beautiful day."

– Unknown

Initially, I had made a chart of what I can and can't do with my ability:

What I Can Do:	What I Can't Do:
Access messages sent from nearby surroundings	Read emojis and other special characters
Read the contact name or phone number that sent the message	Access documents(pdfs, gifs, etc.) attached to a message
	Track messages through game servers

The amount of things from "What I Can't Do" overweighed "What I Can Do." That *needed* to change. I believed after more experience, most of the bullets listed in the "What I Can't Do" section would move to the opposite section.

Some messages had codes in them, which I later found out were emojis in unicode number form. I printed out the unicode numbers for each emoji. Knowing how I learn, it wouldn't take much time to memorize all the codes for each emoji. I found out the emoji that Danny was referring to was a devil smiley face. Something was up.

There were many bilingual people at my middle school, the highest Spanish population out of all. My school Spanish lessons were progressing very slowly, so I asked this dude in my grade called Pablo if he could tutor me after school. Pablo was one of the few kids who knew both Spanish and English. He agreed, but only on specific days, with payment. I couldn't blame him for being demanding. I might have taken some of his free time. I just needed to know what people were saying(in my case, texting) to each other, so that if it was important, then I could translate. And besides, learning a new language was always one of my many aspirations(other than the stupid, insensible ones I had made when I was a child, that I eventually abandoned).

Over the past few days, I've been observing Danny and Will's recent message history. They created a group called, "People of the Plan." No major info had come, just making people join the group. It wasn't until a few days later when Danny posted the "major info" I was looking for:

Hi All,

All of the people here are failing the math tests, and I wanna fix that. Today, we're gonna steal the answer sheet,and not only that, we're gonna breach the freakin' system and steal the online copy using the help of a hired hacker. Any problems? If so, get outta this chat and live your life!

I knew that if somebody within the chat who didn't want to cheat ratted Danny out, he would punish them severely. I just hoped *that* wouldn't happen.

Smitty:

Not at all, Danny. Thanks, dude. [U1F44D]

Giorgio:

[U2705]

Oh, okay. So, *this* was Danny's game. After two years, I could finally *do* something with my messages. I had never expected it to be crime solving, but hey, at least I have a job now. Now I wouldn't need to think of my messages as useless and wonder what I'd do with them. Whoever was in charge of my destiny, thank you for assigning me this. But how would I tackle this problem? I needed more people than myself. Ah-ha! Whoever the person of interest would be… they would need to be a true hacker.

Chapter 4

Vigilante with a Hacker

"Amateurs hack systems; professionals hack people."

– Bruce Schneier

There was only one person that could hack for me and create a fake username: Ernest Dawson. Typical techie, with thick glasses and all(this statement was not meant to be rude, but still, his physical appearance denoted his expertise). The reason our school had no IT person is because Ernest could fix all the computer-related issues for everyone(In fact, the previous IT guy was fired because he couldn't fix the issue when Ernest could). He surely was a hacker. Ernest was an outcast, and didn't really have any friends. This was because of what people called "trust issues." When anyone had befriended Ernest, they would trust him with some of their secrets, which he would reveal. But I somehow knew that he could keep important secrets. His mindset probably thought of embarrassing moments, crushes, and other middle schoolers' stupid secrets as trivial. Hopefully, he'd keep our mission as confidential as he could.

My plan was to create a fake email account, send Danny's message to the school, and eventually, end troubles for many people. I put my third hemisphere aside, and focused on the lessons, occasionally listening in to check on the "People of the Plan" group status. Nothing important so far, which probably meant that they hadn't started their plan yet. Good.

After school, I awkwardly asked Ernest, "Hey, wanna hang out together for a while?" He seemed rather confused, as to why Nathan Bauer, out of nowhere, asks him to chat along with him. I said, "I know, right? We wouldn't typically find ourselves in this situation, but I have something you'd rather like.” His ears perked up like a rabbit, and he finally spoke. “What is it?” he curiously asked. I said, “I want to start a vigilante group together, one that needs some hacking skills.” He looked at me as if I had a tumor in my brain. “No, dude, if it's something as risky as vigilantism, I’m staying out of it.” I said, “Same mentality here, but it’ll also help you. I was added to this group that Danny created, saying that he was going to steal the answer sheet to the math test.” I didn’t want to share my ability with him, of course. If I wasn’t even going to inform my family members, then there wasn’t any point in informing him. Ernest’s sky-blue eyes lit up like LEDs, and adjusted his glasses to look directly at me. “You want to get Danny in trouble for his mistakes, but you want to also be secretive, and make sure nobody knows you reported this incident, hence you confronted me.” I said, “Bingo. I’ll meet you tomorrow at your house, if you're free.” It seemed even he was tired of Danny’s constant bullying and troublesome behavior, and wanted to put an end to it. He replied, “Sure, anytime is fine.” It was humorous how we were so casually planning to get someone in trouble, and how we showed no signs of remorse or anxiety. I knew he would be interested in this activity, because he wrote his address on a sticky note and handed it to me. It read, 3773 APPLE ORCHARD LANE. I got home and added the meeting to my calendar. Powerful skills require proper planning.

I woke up the next morning, quickly eating my oatmeal. I asked my dad, “Dad, I need to review the math test with my friend. Could I go, please?” I knew he wouldn’t deny my request, because it was related to education. Or at least, he *thought* it was related to education. When he agreed, I rode my bike over to Ernest’s house, and knocked on the door. Ernest opened, and said, “Come in. Let’s go to my room.”

Ernest’s teeth clacked along with the keyboard, as he created a fake username. “Would you like it to be MysticVortex34?”

"Too extravagant," I said.

"ShadowBeast99?"

"Too typical."

"KevintheKoolKid15?"

"Are you *really* going to ask me about that one?"

"What about SpectersCloak23?"

That one caught my eye. "Yup, that's the one." After a little more typing, Ernest said, "Okay, it's made. Now you type." I had increased my average typing speed from 50 words per minute to 65 words per minute, so it wouldn't take much time, and I could get my first lesson from Pablo. I started typing:

ADDRESS CLASSIFIED

November 13, 2018

Lloyd Davenport
Livermore Middle School
lloyddavenport@lvjusd.net
3427 Stonehenge Drive
Livermore, CA 94551
Good Morning,

I've come to inform you that one of your students, Daniel Wilson, is going to steal the answer sheet of the 6th Grade Unit 3 Math Test. I was added to this group with the following message:

Danny:

Hi All,

All of the people here are failing the math tests, and I wanna fix that. Today, we're gonna steal the answer sheet,and not only that, we're gonna breach the freakin' system and steal the online copy using the help of a hired hacker. Any problems? If so, get outta this chat and live your life!

Many of the students supported the idea, which makes me suspect that they will be part of the plan. I would like this information between us only.

Regards,
SpectersCloak23
Specterscloak23@gmail.com

I quickly sent the message, without editing spelling or punctuation mistakes, although I thought grammar and all was *pretty* covered. I said, "Bye, Ernest, gotta go back home. Tiresome tutoring." Ernest said hurriedly, "Wait, have this." He opened a bottle of ginger ale, and poured some for both of us. He said, with a smirk, “Cheers to a vigilante team.” and downed the liquid in one gulp. I copied the same, but ended up furrowing my brow at the strong taste of the fizzy substance. I suddenly felt a strange poking at my nose, and I burped. Ernest did so, too. We chuckled. “Yeah, that’s what happens, but you’ll get used to it,” he said. I waved goodbye as I exited the door. I sat on my bike, and journeyed back home to get some Español knowledge from Pablo. I needed to rush. I was already a minute late, and I didn’t know how he would react to tardiness. Hopefully, he won't quit teaching me. I was really interested in learning Spanish. Muy interesante, sin duda.

Chapter 5

Suspension

"As the world we live in is so unpredictable, the ability to learn and adapt to change is imperative, alongside creativity, problem-solving, and communication skills."

- Alain Dehaze

I crossed the street, and walked to my house. I knocked on the door. My mom opened it. "Guten Tag, my son. Your friend, Pablo, is here, ja? So kind of the boy to give Spanish lessons to you. Go and see what he has to say."

I was biracial, my mother German and my father Indian, so we had a lot of mixed traditions we followed, including the fact that I inherited my mom's middle name and my sister inherited my dad's middle name(but my mom insisted on keeping our last name as Bauer, and not Sharma, which my mom and dad are *still* not on good terms about). My father was Hindu, and my mother was Jewish, so our neighbors labeled us as 'Hin-Jews.' Our prayer room consists of the many gods in Hinduism, and the Torah, the holy book of Judaism. We light dias, and menorahs, and celebrate holidays of both traditions. At school, people pronounced my name like "NAY-thun," but at home, my parents pronounced it like "NAH-thun."

My house was a modest, not-too-big, not-too-small area. Thankfully, my parents hold reputable positions, my dad being in the consulting department of a company called Cymbal Financial Services, and my mom a lead scientist in a biotech research facility. That's one of the reasons we lived in a house with a breathable amount of living space. My dad left the house early, and was back a little before I returned from school. My mom had to stay back to keep things ready, and help us awaken from our slumber. She usually came back around five o'clock. Our home had many different types of flooring, none carpet(my parents had decided to remove all carpet in the house shortly after Noah was born, *you can guess why*). Most rooms within the house had varnished wood, and the bathrooms had ceramic tiling. It was a Jewish-styled house, mini chandeliers in the dining room, bidets in the bathrooms, and detailed architectural design on the ceiling. It was a two-story house, the upper level having less square area than the lower. The stairway started one way, then forked two ways. We also had a backyard with a nine-foot-deep pool and a garden. Luckily, my parents got a good deal on the house back in the day. With current inflation, the house prices are just *soaring*. One of my favorite things about the house is that it reflects my culture. For instance, in the stairway, a Hindu statue of Shiva dancing in the form of *Nataraja*. The sculpture was coated with gold, and was adorned with jade. It seemed to fit with our Hin-Jew culture, hence why we put it there. Our house was in a cul-de-sac, one of the many cul-de-sacs of our neighborhood. Behind our house, there were woods, but that was government property, so to *ever* go back there, we needed a permit. I never knew what was beyond the woods, and since we couldn't go back there, I used to call it the "Forbidden Woods," from some inspiration from the Disney movie *Hocus Pocus*. No wonder our street name was "Sherwood Court" (From the Sherwood Forest in *Robin Hood*). Some people found it creepy if you lived in Sherwood Court, but I didn't understand what was so scary about it.

Pablo said, "Five minutes late. Cinco minutos tarde." I said, "Sorry, was visiting a friend. We may begin now." Pablo spent half an hour teaching the lesson, which was probably three whole school Spanish lessons. Very productive. He understood the school's Spanish curriculum, and since we had already finished Unit 1, which was the language basics, he moved on to Unit

2, which was the communication unit. This focused on greeting people, introducing yourself and others, and identifying places in the house, neighborhood, and world. I pulled out the Hamilton and Lincoln I had in my pocket, plus a 20% tip of three extra dollars. It was weird; I was treating my Spanish tutor as a waiter, although I believed the term was called “teacher incentive allotment.” I knew he would be more than happy with the eighteen dollars I gave him. He had received more than what he asked for, and he deserved it. He left soon after thanking me. Suddenly, my sister appeared out of nowhere, with boxing gloves, a Darth Vader helmet, cowboy overalls, a toy sorcerer’s staff, and flip-flops. She said, “Stop in your tracks, trespasser. Describe your activities with this new lad.” I sighed. She would never get over this stuff. “I think it's time you *grow up*, Noemi,” I said. “I was getting Spanish lessons from Pablo, because my Spanish lessons at school are going slow. I have explained myself; now let me go.” My twin sister removed her staff from my way, and let me go. I skipped away, and said, "By the way, your diary is *very* unusual." just to enrage her. She was very possessive about her diary. *Too* possessive, in fact. She screamed, "*YOU* READ MY DIARY!! OH, YOUR DEAD, BRO! D-E-A-D!" She chased me through the house like a cheetah hunting an antelope, and *that* was going to be the last of me. I quickly found a room and locked it. I gasped, "I just did that for fun! I didn't actually read your diary! Geez." Noemi said, "Darn right, you didn't. You knew that you would be the main course for my supper if you had." That was one thing I *also* found annoying, her grotesqueness.

Noemi and I are not just different behaviorally, but physically as well. First off, we are non-identical twins(the "non-identical" already giving it off). Second, Noemi has a dark skin tone like my dad, and I have a light skin tone similar to my mom. I have sea-green eyes, while Noemi has chocolate-brown eyes. Since the fourth grade, I have been wearing glasses, unlike Noemi. I don't wear it too often, because it only occurs when I stare at a device. The doctors prescribed me the glasses, thinking that I needed to wear them all the time, because the eye exam was done on a small TV. When I got my glasses two weeks after the test was done, the doctors were puzzled as to why the glasses only worked when I was in front of an electronic device. It started around the same time my third hemisphere formed, so they probably were related. Nowadays, many of the assignments in school are digital, so I have to use my glasses then. It really helped complete my character as a nerdy, short sixth-grader, because what was a nerd, without his glasses? When we were toddlers, we pretended that each other never existed, worrying our parents as to how twins could be so different. But one thing that I wondered is if Noemi had also inherited my ability. She seemed fine at school; nothing looked as if something disturbed her. I kept convincing myself that she couldn't have it, that she would react differently to it. I mean, we are *so* different, so it's likely she wouldn't have it, right? I looked at a clock in the room. It was thirty minutes to dinner. Just enough time to practice violin. I walked towards the room that had my violin, and sat down to practice. I sighed. At least no scoldings from my orchestra teacher.

The next day at school, I was finished with history class, and was walking towards math class when the following announcement was heard on the PA:

Daniel Wilson, please report to the front office, Daniel Wilson.

I pumped my fist in the air for joy. My plan worked! I caught up with Ernest, who was walking towards Honors Math, and gave him a high five. "Plan success," I said. Ernest grinned at me, and we went our ways.

Rumors were whispered in every hallway about Danny. Some said he was temporarily suspended, some exaggerated, and said he was expelled. Many other people from the group were called, but were pardoned of punishment after explaining themselves. One girl had actually listened to the conversation, and soon, word didn't spread about Danny, but my username. "*SpectersCloak23? Cool.*"

Oh my gosh, he sounds so hot, whoever he is!"

"*Who could it be? Is it a boy or girl? Mysterious.*"

It was cool to be so famous. Even though I didn't want attention, I found this indirect attention very influential. I thanked Ernest later, "Thank you for all of this. Even though I'm not the guy who wants fame, I do admit, I could learn to like this feeling." Ernest said, "Same. See you around, dude. Bye." I waved at him, and he got on the bus. I took my bike out of the bicycle parking, and rode back home, feeling… useful, at the same time powerful. This was what I found was missing in all the time I have had my power. This feeling. Now, I was able to use my power to contribute.

But I was missing many things, of course. I needed more control and more awareness. These were the things that would fill me(not my stomach, my internal self). And here I was, enjoying a nice autumn breeze, whistling a jolly tune as I entered my neighborhood seated atop my cycle.

I had realized that I could not only stop other people's problems within school, but people that are closer to me. My friend, Ethan, was a close family friend. In fact, we were born alongside each other in the hospital. My mom decided to name me Nathan, so his mom named him Ethan. He had curly brown hair, brown eyes, and a cut near his eyebrow. Every time I went over to his house for a sleepover, I would strangely intercept messages late in the night.

Cinema Scrimmage 3D:

You have unlocked Level 10: Jafar! Congrats! Play now to unlock Level 11: Hades!!

I would think, "*Why would he get gaming messages this late in the night?*" Then, I would just shrug it off, and go back to sleep. But then the amount of messages started to increase exponentially. I had eavesdropped on his parents talking to him about his grades dropping. I had noticed him always with drowsy, red eyes with dark circles under them. Since we went to the same school, and shared our Math Honors class, I saw him sleep off, and Mrs. Gowda had to keep reprimanding him. Soon, I had to confirm my suspicions. I went to his parents, and told them about my discovery(of course, without disclosing my power), and asked them to look into it. Since they had been seeing his grades drop, they believed that it could be because of his gaming addiction. Thankfully, his parents helped him recover from it, and he was now back on track. My power did have its pros and cons, but I can still let it help people.

Chapter 6

The Online Policeman

"Being a good tattle-tale requires exceptional attention to details and then blowing them out of proportion."

- Unknown

I had been seeing some strange things lately. There were many kids with green hoodies and many chalk and graffiti messages saying "WE SUPPORT YOU" and "YOU HELP US." I didn't have a clue of what was going on, some new school tradition, perhaps? I found out why when I came to the west wall of the school. The colorful, abstract writing said:

THANK YOU, SPECTER

So, all of this was for *me*. Me. A random guy from 6th grade. Actually, not really me. Ernest was the one who created SpectersCloak23. Many people's signatures adorned the graffiti. I decided to sign too, just so that nobody suspected me. I'll ask Ernest to do so later. Now, I *just* need to get to first period.

I was anxiously waiting as the math teacher passed out the math test. When she came to my desk, she said, "Good job, Mr. Bauer." I carefully gazed down at my paper, and a big "100" was written at the top left corner. I sighed with relief. My average 98 in math will now become a 99. The startling bell rang, and I shoved my test into my folder and walked toward orchestra class. I had been spending more time playing violin, so I felt pretty confident now. If that painful rough draft during the fifth period wouldn't be there, then I would have been living the best day ever. No messages, no meddling, all peace.

Today, in my ELAR class, a troublesome kid by the name of Bill got in a *serious* hassle with the teachers(hence why I mentioned the word "troublesome"). My *fate* is such that he was *my* tablemate. You can imagine my sorry plight, such a pain he was. He would torment me daily with rhymes like, "My name is Bill, not as stupid as Phil, always gotta chill, Bill, Bill. Not the science guy, not a teensy bit shy, Bill, Bill. Liquor is Bill, tough to distill, Bill, Bill." And he would forcefully slap me on the back during the song as if I was some sort of drum. He would always create scenes in class, causing my ELAR teacher to always redden up like a tomato every time he was problematic. No wonder her hair had started to gray. In middle school, there would always be kids who were not really good, and to me, that was okay. There would be some biodiversity, to put it, in a school ecosystem. But this Bill *kills.* Today, he walked into the room angry, growling at kids who talked to him(I think he was about to bite too, but that could have been from the way he bared his outwardly crooked, buck-toothed teeth). He yelled at Ms. Lynn, who was forced to call the office after he made some threatening statements and was about to poke somebody in the eye with a pen. Of course, he earned a demerit. Demerits were basically the opposite of merits; you would earn them for bad behavior, even tardies. The school hosted many events, and there were a certain number of demerits, usually twelve, which were the basis of your attendance to these events(which explains why Bill usually never came to the school parties). There were steps to get these demerits, with the first being a verbal warning, the second receiving a Stop-and-Think form, and the third filling out the form, officially earning the demerit. "*If the bad behavior continues, then the teacher will call the admin, and that student will have an office referral,*" I remember the counselor saying in a presentation to the entire grade level. You would earn specific detentions and suspensions based on the amount of demerits, except for some cases, like Danny's. The thing he did was deserving of suspension and only *suspension*. Well, Bill was brought to the office, he was talked to, and I had heard from some people that he was just having a tough time at home. The final result hadn't come out yet(whether he would be suspended or not), but I decided I shouldn't focus on all these things.

Me and Ernest had been preventing more bad stuff in school. There was an eighth grader who was threatening Ernest, so we asked some other bully victims and found out that this bully does swirlies to people in the bathroom. We started putting mini wall cameras in the boys' bathroom and sent an email to the principal containing a video of the bully harassing a boy. The next day, suspension. I didn't want to go too deep into crime-fighting, like stopping drugs and guns in the school, but we decided that it was worth it. We listened in on drug carriers and dealers at school and "reported" to the principal. Who knew that we'd find "online tattle-telling" fun?

The principal organized an assembly, and asked, "Now, as you all may know, I am getting messages about certain people's bad behavior from an anonymous account named *SpectersCloak23*," he explained, with a slight tone of sternness in his voice. Certain people's nostrils flared. Some people were mad at me for suspending their friends. Well, too bad, so sad. He continued, "I, and other people, I assume, want to know who is responsible for this." His eyes narrowed. "*Who* created the account?" Actually, the truth was, Ernest created the account, and I typed the emails, so even we weren't sure who he was referring to. We kept our faces casual and sat silent with the rest of the assembly. The principal straightened his posture. "Very well then, if any of you receives any information regarding who created the account, please let me know. You may all go to your classrooms." He walked away from the stage as the classes walked away, isolating the auditorium. The irony was that nobody would tell the principal, even if they found out who did it(whether it be false or true), because nobody wanted to look like a tattle-tale. And why was the principal so insecure and aggravated about our reporting? Wasn't he supposed to feel the opposite, because I was helping him stop the bad stuff happening within the school? I needed to listen to the principal's messages, just for info. Eh, I could take this tension after Thanksgiving Break. My family was going to Laguna Beach. So, lots of *other* things to think about. Every human being *needs* some entertainment. That's just how it works!

Later that day, I was called from my class to the assistant principal's office. People were randomly being pulled from their classes, and I didn't know why. I never heard about it, nor did I sense any messages about it. Well, I guess I'd find out now. I walked in tension, then sighed as I looked at the name on the assistant principal’s door:

ERICA DOMINUS,

ASSISTANT PRINCIPAL

In Livermore Middle School, *all* the students were big fans of Ms. Dominus. She was kind, optimistic, and listened to everyone’s opinions. Her charisma not only worked on students but teachers, too. Principal Davenport, a man whose primary focus wasn’t on the school, would show a degree of submission to Ms. Dominus, which either proved she was a mystique master or had an unknown level of authority over the principal. Her burgundy hair had slight streaks of gold, and her amber eyes always glinted playfully. Ms. Dominus lived on the road parallel to the children's park, where you would see more costly homes of celebrities and athletes. I was surprised that a teacher with a single income could have so much money. Probably inherited.

Chill, Nathan, don't freak out, I said to myself as I timidly knocked on the door. *You're probably not in trouble.* The door opened, and I saw the warm smile of Ms. Dominus. "Hello, Nathan, come on in!" she said, cheerful and vibrant. "Don't worry, you aren't in trouble. I just have a few questions for you." She led me into a conference room, and there I saw the principal and a school police officer. I wasn't sure what her name was. I gulped. *Did I do anything? Did I witness anything I wasn't supposed to?* Then it struck me. SpectersCloak23. I was sure they didn't know who it was because then why would they bring in other people? "Hello, Nathan." the principal said, his tone serious. "There can be nothing better than stopping the injustices that are occurring unbeknownst to the authorities, but foreign influence and interference is not welcome within Livermore Middle, hence why I organized the assembly and are doing individual student interviews," he explained. "Now, do you have any whereabouts or information regarding the identity of SpectersCloak23?"

"No," I tried to lie with ease. "I only started hearing about him recently, and I haven't been a part of any such activities in the school, so he hasn't ever contacted me."

The police officer took some notes on her paper. Hopefully, she wasn't skilled in reading faces. "Can you tell us the last time you heard somebody talk about SpectersCloak23, and who that person was?" The officer asked. I read her name tag. Brooklynn Campbell. I thought about it for a while. Lots of people were talking about him(or, well, Ernest and I), and I just selected somebody at random. "Chase Lin. He is in my orchestra class. I first heard about SpectersCloak23 from him two days ago." Officer Campbell jotted down some more notes. "Do you know any bully victims that have or haven't any of their incidents reported by SpectersCloak23?" Ms. Dominus asked. Whew. This was like the crime shows with the interrogations and stuff. “No, I am not aware of any individual that has been bullied.” I lied, trying not to show any microexpressions that contradicted my statements. I hoped that Ernest would do the same and stay safe. “If you receive any information regarding SpectersCloak23’s whereabouts, please do contact us at the tip line. You are free to return to your class once you submit a written statement of what you have told us.” the principal said. Officer Campbell said, “Thank you for your cooperation, Sir,” and Ms. Dominus gave me a smile and a small pat on the back. “I know, pretty intimidating, right?” she said. I let out a small laugh. “Yeah, definitely,” I said as I put my words to the paper. After a minute, I handed the paper over to Ms. Dominus, and she wrote me a pass back to class. Phew! Now, I won’t be associated with SpectersCloak23. I prayed for Ernest. But at least that’s some tension off my back before Thanksgiving break.

Chapter 7

A Tension Arises

"Conflict grows out of ignorance and suspicion."

– Gordon B. Hinckley

A FEW DAYS LATER
NOVEMBER 19, 2018

I asked Ernest about the interrogation, and he said he also gave his false statements with caution and diverted the suspicion, which gave us a ton of relief.

We had already packed our bags and filled the car's gas the night before, so the moment Noemi and I came back from school the Friday before the break, we got into the car to start our Thanksgiving journey. We drove for four hours straight until we reached Santa

Clarita. There, we met my mom's close friend Linda, her husband Axel, and their daughters Lisbet and Emilie. We stayed there for the night and enjoyed their hospitality. Since Lisbet, Emilie, and Noemi pretended like I didn't exist when I was in their presence, I decided to act the same way. There were some interesting books in their house, and it was always a pleasure to talk to Mr. and Mrs. Becker, so I didn't have to sit in tension and be weird. The next morning, we drove for two hours to reach Laguna Beach and checked into our hotel. After putting our stuff in the room, we came downstairs to have breakfast. So, I started my day off with two waffles, one croissant, some fruits, and a glass of orange juice. After the flavorsome meal, we rode the elevator back to our room, 508. After we got settled in again, I turned on the shower, and water started drizzling over my head. I scrubbed the bubbly soap over my body, got one squirt of the fragrant aloe vera shampoo, and rubbed it on my hair. After a good fifteen minutes in the shower, my feet shifted from the blue-tiled floor of the shower to the walnut-colored floor of the bathroom. I brushed myself with a nearby towel and then applied some moisturizer. I had eczema while growing up, so after I shower, I put on some body lotion or moisturizer, as recommended by my pediatrician, Dr. Arzney. Whenever I went to a hotel room, I made sure to find body lotion. I searched for some clothes and found a blue T-shirt that depicted an alien, and black jeans. After I put them on, I exited the bathroom, and there was *my* sister putting something in the safe. Very likely, her diary. Although I've never read her diary, I had the urge to, because I wanted to know if I could find out if she had my skills, but I'd have to do it during the night so that Noemi doesn't know.

The time on the alarm clock read 10:32. Feeling bored, I opened my book up to the next chapter and began reading. *The Iliad*, a classic indeed. Eventually, as I finished the book, the time was 5:35, and we decided to head down to the beach.

I wore jazzy green sunglasses, a loose beach shirt, and some khaki shorts. Noemi wore an orange swimsuit. Noemi wasn't interested in going to the beach for a sunset and instead wanted to play in the ocean. I am not the type to go to the beach for water fun. I would sit along the shore, sipping some juice of sorts, like that one I had at Ernest's house. Ginger ale, I think. I liked the way the flavor and the fizz worked hand-in-hand in my mouth. Dad and I would be relaxing at the shore, while Mom and Noemi would be swimming and jet skiing. The apparel differences in the family would make people think that we're not related at all. But let them do what they want to do. If I was going to enjoy it, then that's what mattered. Dad brought his guitar, patted me on the back, and we headed out.

The beach exceeded my expectations. It was *so* peaceful. The palm trees swayed rhythmically in the breeze, and the number of people was also very minimal. *Just* what I wanted. We sat down, and stared at the sky for some time. Dad asked me general questions about school, and we chuckled over the many humorous events in life. As we saw the sun lowering its position and the pink swirls blending into the honey-gold sky, my dad began a song. I did wonder why he had brought the guitar in the first place.

'♪ We're sittin' on the shore ♪'
'♪ Gazing at the sky ♪'
'♪ Enjoyin' the breeze ♪'
'♪ Attempting to fly ♪'
'♪ Let's say hi to the blushing clouds ♪'

He strummed a little more, and then stood up, and bowed. I clapped for him, grinning. My dad was drawn to the magic of guitar ever since he came to America. So, he started to learn it. After a couple of years, he was probably in a competition with street musicians! "It's all about passion," he once told me. "That's the masala, or spice, in the music that gives it clarity and essence. And to put it simply, clarity and essence is the 'life' of the music." That's why my violin sucks. There is no passion. The problem was, I really didn't have any interest in playing the violin. I liked most varieties of music, although I didn't prefer to express it using a violin. I simply had to select something between orchestra, band, or choir as an elective. We played in the sand, the tiny grains stuck between our toes. We searched for crabs, either dormant inside a shell or crawling in the wet sand near the seashore. When the sky turned dim, and little splotches of stars started to appear, we called it a night and headed back to the resort. Mom and Noemi followed shortly after us, completely drenched, with a purple towel draped around them. While they took a shower, my dad ordered from an Indian restaurant. Then, we started by crunching on some samosas and dipping them in chutney. It was a little spicy, but I was able to manage. My dad devoured the food voraciously. He must have loved the food(particularly because it was Indian street food and probably tasted exactly how he wanted), although my mom made Indian cuisine too(along with Thai, Mexican, German, Indochinese, etc.) We were vegetarian, particularly because of my father's tradition. My mom used to eat non-veg food before, but soon adapted to my dad's tradition. I had a neutral opinion about vegetarianism vs. meat-eating. If the people of the world kept eating meat, then vegetable prices would continue to remain cheap. I respected the animals of the world and didn't want to cause them harm. I was allowed to eat eggs, but I didn't really like the taste. I was okay with it in cakes and other things, though. I received many questions about vegetarianism over the years, and I was fed up with the amount of them that were repeated(sometimes by the same people). Fortunately, in middle school, nobody cared about what diet people followed, because there were way too many kids who didn't care. In elementary, you had much fewer kids and classes, so there was more likelihood of nosy curiosity. I do remember we had gone to a vegetarian restaurant called “Bloodless” a year ago. When I heard the name, I started to taste iron in my mouth. The concept of that restaurant was that everything was meat, but plant-based. My mom was excited, particularly because she hadn’t had meat in a long time, and wanted to see what plant-based meat tasted like. My dad was curious to have meat for the first time, without feeling the caution or doubt he once had. My sister didn’t really care; she was just hungry that day. I had a doubt she must have had meat sometime(like when she had bought lunch from the school cafeteria in kindergarten, even when my mom had packed her food), but that was probably me just being paranoid. She was already scolded for that back then, and she learned from her mistake. She had told us she didn’t buy any sort of meat whatsoever. We went to the restaurant, and I was so disgusted with the weird textures that I almost puked. My dad munched on it for a little while and got used to the food. Noemi didn’t care, and served herself multiple times, finished her plate, and gave a loud belch after that(and instead of a polite "Excuse me," she said, "That was some *good* stuff.") One of our family morals was to never waste food, but my mom saw that I just couldn't take it. I guess if I had eaten it for a few months, I would have gotten used to it. So, she ate whatever was left on my plate, and we left the place. At home, she then gave me some curd rice and some *dal* to fill me since I couldn't eat the restaurant food. That day, I had taken a good decision to always stick to natural veg food and not really explore these *other* options.

The rice arrived on the dinner table. *Arroz*, I remember Pablo saying while teaching me food names in Spanish. I said, "*Nosotros comemos arroz.*" which seemed to completely stupefy my family. Noemi's brow raised above her head, and Dad dropped his fork on his plate. Mom said, with a big smile, "Wow, that Pablo friend of yours is being very effective, ah? Why do you all look like Nathan regurgitated slugs? He's learning Spanish, my boy!" and gave me a *big, wet* smooch on the cheek. I immediately wiped it off with my napkin, although my mom didn't seem to notice. We resumed eating, and finished soon after. The discussion during supper wasn't the usual dramatic kind, just some small talk here and there. Then, when we switched off the lights and I heard the soft snoring of my dad, I decided to make my move. I got off the bed, tip-toed to the closet, and opened it. There was the small, black safe sitting right over the mini-fridge. My mom's brows creased, and she twitched an ear. "Nathan, what are you doing?" she asked drowsily. I stopped, my heart thumping. I said casually, "Nothing, Mom, just getting some water." I tried to open the safe, but it was latched together like glue. I tried punching in some numbers, like her birthday, our address, but failed. Somehow, the beeps coming from the safe didn't affect everybody's slumber. I gave up, and I actually opened the fridge and took a slurp of water. I suddenly was hit with something: *a message*. It happened so rarely nowadays that I almost forgot about it.

Unknown User:

Truck's loaded. Supply is high. Pharma will work out.

Boss:

Good. We'll meet in the lobby.

Unknown User:

Aye, Cap.

I knew these people were getting their hands into something dirty; that was clear. The only thing so confusing about the conversation was, "Pharma will work out." What was *that* supposed to mean? Were they selling something to the pharmaceutical industry, *something* illegal? Who knew? Maybe I could do something about this. But all I knew was it's 9:30, and I needed to sleep, so I closed the fridge, walked back to my bed, and snuggled in, my thoughts slowly drifting away.

Chapter 8

Dangerous Dreams

“They’ve promised us that dreams come true– but forgot to mention that nightmares are dreams, too.”

- Oscar Wilde

My eyes slowly opened, yet I couldn’t see anything, because of an itchy fabric draped over my head. My hands and legs were tied, binded by thick rope. The room was swelteringly hot, and I felt like dousing my body in a frozen lake. And my thirst, my parched throat, had a desperate need to have even a drop of water. The bag over my head was removed, and my vision faded into view. I saw a dim light dangling over my head, and my feet were resting on a dusty floor. I was in a narrow room, which made me feel a little claustrophobic. A tall man in a gray army suit sat in a chair in front of me, his blond locks neatly combed over his head. He got up from his chair and circled me, his polished boots tapping the floor. “So…” he drew out slowly, “are you planning to tell us?” with a thick accent. I said, “I don’t know what you are talking about.” He nodded, lit a pipe, and stuck it between his lips. He took a whip and started to lash it on the ground. He said, “You know very well what I’m talking about. About your exceeded knowledge in connections. So I just want to know about your country’s internal affairs, maybe some warfare logistics if needed, and back to your normal life.” I was shocked. He knew. He knew about my abilities. And yet I didn’t utter a word. He began to thrash me, the hard leather beating against my skin. The pain was unbearable. He said, “It doesn’t have to be like this. Just say it.” Instead, I spat on his face, and he winced with disgust. He said, “My wife has her interests in gardening, so I suppose this is her inspiration.” He took a pair of pruners from a metal tray and placed my index finger between them. I jolted and yelled as the blades sunk into my finger and snapped it off, falling to the ground. My hand twinged in pain, and I wheezed, “I still won’t tell.” At this point, he was tired of my adamant behavior, and said, “I just don’t know why the lower class doesn’t understand anything.” He took out his pistol and cocked his gun, aimed straight for my head. He fired. My life whirred past my eyes as the bullet traveled to me…

My eyes popped open, and my hand quivered. I try to relax. Just a dream, I thought. Drool trickled down my cheek. I got up and went to wash my face, then brushed my teeth. I asked why we were not going down for breakfast, and my parents told me that we were going to Panera Bread for brunch. Oh, great. I was so hungry I could eat Godzilla’s mass in food. I sighed, and plopped down on a couch. I thought about yesterday night. Who could this Unknown User be? Or Boss? Foof, it’s a lot of thinking. Could they just be pharmacists on vacation who were talking about a huge product sale?

But in the coy way they were conversing, the chances of that were slim. My dad’s phone buzzed in his pocket, and he said, “Time for brunch.” I exhaled with relief. My hunger would be satisfied. I stuck my feet into my slippers and had a new joy in my stride. After all, who wouldn't be happy to have a bite of food after a late morning?

As I sunk my teeth deep into the sandwich, I thought about the conversation I heard, or rather sensed. It had been on my mind for quite a while now, and my mom seemed to notice. She frowned, and said, “Food is enjoyable, and is supposed to be cherished, so wipe that foul look off your face and enjoy your sandwich.” I managed to put a smile on and took a bite out of my sandwich, the juice of the vegetables inside filling my mouth, and gulped it. Then I asked for the autumn squash soup, and I poured myself some. After loading our stomachs with sandwiches and soups, we decided to have an afternoon nap. “You know, sleep during the daytime reduces the chances of heart disease,” Dad pointed out. Noemi rolled her eyes and bounced onto the mattress next to mine. I simply said, “I’ll sleep on the couch. It’s comfy enough.” hoping for a better dream. I took a pillow and a blanket and set up my area while everybody else got on the beds. I closed my eyes and let myself drift off into wherever my mind will take me…

I stood, observing the setting around me. A long wall towered over me, and army tents were set up everywhere. Men in heavy armor went inside and outside different tents, retrieving newly-forged weapons. A man walked up to me, the same outfit everyone was wearing. He has a silky black beard and a tight bun on the top of his head. The bun has a talisman that goes through it, and something made me think he was the commander. He started to speak to me in a foreign language that seemed to be Chinese. I said, in English, “Sorry, Sir, I did not understand.”

He says, “Oh, you speak English? I speak little, but try to understand,” he gestures. “Time very little, and I need help. I need your power to give me knowledge about the Mongols. We battle them and need to know how strong. I give you money if you want.” I say, also in broken English, “No need for money. Will help you.” A smile breaks across his face, and he speaks words of gratitude in his language. When he tries to explain, I say, “I understood.” He yells to his men and raises a palm to signify, “Wait.”

“Nathan,” a soft voice calls out from the cloudy sky. No one seems to notice. “Nathan!” the voice calls louder.

Something shakes my shoulder, and then I realize I’m dreaming.

I opened my eyes to see Mom hovering over me, waiting for me to wake up. “Oh, thank god you woke up; I was about to splash water on you.” I saw Noemi with her diary, and I almost forgot that I needed to check it. I peer at the passcode she enters on the safe: 0002. Her password was very basic, but smart. Nobody would guess such a common number, even though it was common. As Noemi enters the bathroom, I quickly punch in the code and open the safe. I quickly browsed through her diary, afraid she would come out any second. All her entries were mainly about how sad, angry, or annoyed she felt, or it was about boys she liked, and other times, I read about how I irritated her. I put the book back and re-entered the code just in the nick of time. My mom said, "We are leaving sometime soon today." I whined, "Mom, really, this soon? I thought the break would end in, like, five days or something." My mom replied, "You are right, but you are not aware of the reason." I thought about possible reasons but didn't think that they were the ones. "We received a message from your brother, Noah," my dad filled in. "He's coming to visit for Thanksgiving." Oh. I was surprised that possibility escaped my mind. Well, it would be fun to have Noah over. The more the merrier, I suppose.

Chapter 9

The Attention Grabber

"Brothers aren't simply close; they are knit together."

– Robert Rivers

Noah, my elder brother, had left the house recently to do his pre-med. He was only sixteen, and after accumulating many college and high school credits at an early age, he got to skip two grades. You can understand how his aspiration to be a doctor reflects his personality. Clean, polished, and smart. He was also the tallest in both my mom's and dad's family and had the light skin-tone of my mother but the dark hair and eyes of my father. I had hoped that one day, I'd be as tall as him. Since Noah was such a good child while growing up, he was the center-of-attention during his time at the house, which meant that Noemi and I could do mischief(Well, for me, “mischief” meant experimenting with things in the kitchen and leaving a big mess, and for Noemi, it meant stealing toys, breaking things, making a mess, and even doing a self-haircut). After my parents understood these extremities, they started to pay more attention to what we were doing and scolded us when we were caught. I quickly corrected my bad habits, but it took some time for Noemi to. We are much more helpful and less of a pain than before. Now, my parents don’t really pay much attention to what we do since we were disciplined enough(with Noah being the example child).

I had almost forgotten that if we were going to leave now, then I needed to get some of the unique flavors of soft drinks they sold here in the vending machine. I said hurriedly, “Be back in a sec, Mom,” and quickly ran away before my mother had a chance to respond. I took out some of my savings and paid for the drinks. The drinks moved from their stationary positions behind the rings and slid to the pull-out. I rushed back to our room and knocked on the door.

A gruff voice yelled, “Who’s there?!”

The door creaked open. A man with bangs covering his eyes and an invasive potbelly opened the door. He had a T-shirt that said, “**BEER IS LIFE**.” Clearly, *this* was the wrong room.

He growled, “What do ya’ want, kid?”

I stammered, “S-Sorry, wrong person.”

He slammed the door in my face, and I didn’t take that personally. But still, a guy with superpowers deserves some respect.

We were at home, unpacking all our luggage and sorting out the groceries, when the doorbell rang. My dad was quick to say, “I’ll get it.” We continued to unpack as I heard the door open, and a manly voice said, “Hi, Dad.” I looked up and saw a familiar face embrace Dad. Noah. He had come. He was always so punctual, precise, and disciplined(there were times in which he would act a little childish, like when it was a matter of his pride, but nobody saw his faults) that you could call him "The Golden Boy." Noemi and I have always looked up to Noah as a role model when growing up, not only because our parents used him as an example but because he always got all the attention. As I grew, I understood I can be more productive by myself, and that I don't need my parents to focus on what I do.

Mom walked up to Noah and gave him a huge kiss on the cheek. "It's been so long since I saw you," she said nostalgically. His gaze fell on me, and he said, "Hey bro, what's up?" I said with a smile, "Nothing much; glad you're here." He said, "Also, this is for you." He took out a wrapped box from his suitcase and gave it to me. I thanked him for the gift, surprised that he had the time to think about me and give me something. He called out for Noemi, and she looked at him sternly. He laughed and then said, “I know you used to like mix-and-match costumes, so I bought you a couple.” Out of his bag came three costumes: Captain Marvel, The Mandalorian, and a plague doctor. Noemi exclaimed elatedly, “Thank you so much! I have *always* wanted these ones!” Noah replied, “My pleasure,” with a charming smile. I decided to open my present. It was an anatomy model. I mean, really? Did I *really* want fake guts as a present? But I knew to accept my gifts with gratitude, so I saw the positive side to getting an anatomy model. I could learn more about the medical field using this. As Noemi went to try out her new costumes, I checked the date. Four days till school. The break just has to end.

My family didn’t only include Noah, Noemi, Mom, and Dad. They were simply my home family, or rather, my primary family. On my father’s side, there were my Dada and Dadi, or grandfather and grandmother(“Dada” and “Dadi” is not to be confused with “Dad.” Dad is an American way to address your father, and is pronounced with a short *a*. “Dada” and “Dadi” have a soft *d*, like the “*th*” in “the.” In this case, the pronunciation of *a* is an “ah” sound, and the *i* is an “ee.” Quick pronunciation lesson that will be useful later on). My Dada was a calm, frail man who abided by traditions and wasn’t very happy with my father’s marriage. But he still interacted with my mom, me, and my siblings, as we still followed the Hindu customs. My Dadi, she was *much* different than Dada; she was a talkative, easy-going, life-enjoying lady. She would often say, “Why worry when I have nothing to lose? Ha!” She would rant about her past experiences and laugh with us, play games with us(she was a true card-sharp and would win every card game we played), and enjoy food(which ended up with my Mom being flattered). My dad also had a sister named Anita, but Noah, Noemi, and I would just call her Aunty *ji*. My mom’s parents I knew as Opa and Oma. Opa was very interested in politics and was clear on his views on anything. He was a stout, proper man with greyish-orange hair and a thick mustache. My grandparents were born three years before World War II ended and had to live under tough circumstances to survive as a Jew. My Opa told me stories of how he narrowly escaped being sent off to the camps. I couldn't even imagine being in his circumstances. Thankfully, the Holocaust ended, and Nazi Germany fell. My Oma was peaceful, like my Dada, but had different opinions and morals. She loved flowers, gardening(hence why my dad got along with her so well), books, and embroidery. She liked anything colorful, whether that be literally or figuratively. She had light wrinkles that highlighted her long life, as well as silver streaks in her brown hair. Opa and Oma had been childhood friends during the aftermath of the war. They got married in 1978, and my mom was born two years later. When my mom was in her twenties, she went to the U.S. for college education; she met my dad, and they got married, blah, blah, blah; my siblings and I were born, and life has continued ever since. My dad had many cousins, and so did my mom, and we rarely got to meet them. We met them during special occasions in both families. Since they had kids too, we would all gather together and “play.” Many of my cousins weren’t really too excited to meet each other, and after our parents asked us to go play in a room, we would divide the room into sections for each group. The borders were so strict that commotions frequently occurred over who had crossed the lines. Since I was one of the “older” cousins, my duty was to manage them. That headache would only last a day or two, though. There were two main people involved in destroying the peace and instigating the conflict between the portions of the room. Shree, a bossy eight-year-old with small pigtails that resembled the horns of the devil after you met her, and Pankaj, a greedy-for-toys five-year-old with a lisp. Pankaj, or Panku as we would affectionately call him, would often cross the borders to try and play with other toys, and Shree would start battling with him for breaking the rules. The most violent interaction I had caught between the two was them wrestling. It was so intense I had to call Noemi to come and separate Shree’s tight grip on Panku. Of course, we had to go to their parents and report what had happened. Naveen Chacha would sit and adore his dear son, while Bindu Chachi would reprimand her daughter strictly. Maybe that’s where Shree got her dangerous qualities from. This was on my dad’s side. The terrors on my mom’s side were Walter, a pampered, mischievous blonde, and Miles, Walter’s sidekick from my Opa’s side of the family. They would constantly irritate or play an annoying prank on the rest of my cousins, which caused an unpleasant overlap of high-pitched kid voices. I know they have tried to prank my older cousins, Noemi and I, but we saw through their attempts to try to light our fuse. When Noah came, he was kindly greeted by our uncles, aunts, and cousins. Noah always had a charm on younger kids and could always settle a brawl with a simple request. He never had to be rude or strict, like Noemi and I(just to be clear, Noemi was the rude one, not me). We always were grateful to have him around one of the family gatherings. Whew. My uncles and aunts are generally pleasant to meet, but I still was grateful when my troublesome cousins said their goodbyes. Thankfully, both families weren't the kind that allowed their kids to have devices, and I didn't get any messages from them. I could at least have some other form of tension. I needed to have no tension at all. I didn't know of a way to rid myself of my ability, so I just needed to live with it and maintain it in a way that I would be calm. Sometimes my cousins called, or we called for birthday and holiday wishes. There was a big WhatsApp group for my dad's family, called "Sharma Parivar," and my mom's family, "Bauer Family." I would get messages from either group, particularly more on my mom's side, even though there were fewer people in her family. Knowing I had many relatives in different places around the world made me feel more secure. If I became a lab rat and had a chance to escape, I would go to one of their places. I hoped since I had so many that, whoever was doing the lab tests on me didn't waste time searching. That would be horrible if I was on the run all my life. I would be like that plane that went missing when I was in first gradeu. MH370, the plane owned by Malaysian Airlines, had somehow disappeared from the radar, and to this day, no one knows what exactly happened, although there have been many theories. After watching the news during this horrible time, we were scared to travel by flight anywhere. Speaking of which, if I disappeared, could I be tracked somehow? Was there some sort of microchip in my brain that allowed me to sense text messages, and could that microchip be tracked? That was a possibility, but I shouldn't think about *every* possible scenario. I'd end up in a mental hospital if I continued to think about all the crazy predictions of what would happen. I needed to focus on the present and cool down. Stay on task, resolve problems that come your way, and use your skills to your benefit.

These were the three rules that would help me survive and live long. Other individuals *would* end up in an asylum, become experimental test subjects, or do something that caused harm if they had my ability. Thankfully, I was quite smart enough to manage it well. Maybe.

Chapter 10

Friend, or Foe?

"A friend to honesty and a foe to crime."
– Allan Pinkerton

4 DAYS LATER
NOVEMBER 29, 2018

Here I was, at school, walking towards history class. Things with Noah had been good. We filled him in on what was going on here in Livermore. He left yesterday evening, and everything was back to business. I got my history books out of my backpack, quickly opened my notebook, and started to scribble in notes as Mr. Volkov began his lecture.

"Flip your textbook to page 262 and start reading along with me. The Industrial Revolution," he announced. “The Industrial Revolution was an age of innovation, where machines had started to develop. One example of this is the steam engine, probably one of the most famous and useful inventions of this time period. Another example is the telegraph, invented by Samuel Morse, which sparked the development of long-distance communication during the early 19th century.” As I took in this information, I realized this is very convenient in my case. If I could enhance my ability by expanding my range of seeing notifications, I could get more information on the fishy activity that was going on in the hotel.

Math, orchestra, and science passed by. When it came to language arts, we had to edit our rough draft. I was stumped and did not know what words to add and remove. I always found the writing process very tedious, when you could just get started on the final draft.

Unfortunately, the teacher was going to grade our corrections to the essay. So, I decided to consult the Sinowski brothers. Norbert, Albert, Gilbert, and Robert Sinowski. Norbert was in eighth grade, Albert was in seventh grade, and Gilbert and Robert were twins in my grade. The reason people went to them for help in writing was because their literacy grades are 100, 100, 100, and 100, respectively. Clearly, these were the people who could help me in need. Norbert had thick brown hair, and he never used to wear shorts to school, even during the summer, which I found interesting. He mainly wrote persuasive and argumentative essays. Albert was relatively similar to Norbert, but he had blonde highlights in his hair and was more scrawnier. He specialized in narratives. Gilbert had thick green glasses and braces, and he was obsessed with comics. He was a master at writing science fiction and horror stories, although his writing included many violent elements, which got him in trouble most of the time. Robert, the youngest, aspired to be a software engineer. He wrote informational essays. This week, it was an imaginative essay, and I had written it in the science fiction genre, called "The Bio Bigotry." I had to ask my least favorite of the Sinowski brothers. Gilbert.

He was such a creep, and nobody liked to be near him. "Hello, Nathan," he said eerily as I approached him. "How can I be of *service?*" He smacked his lips and licked them.

I said uneasily, "Yeah, *hi*, Gilbert, can you help me with my science fiction essay? I happen to know you're an expert at it." He replied back with a confident yet freaky face, "Indeed, I do write science fiction. What's your story about? Aliens that consume Gila monsters and eat them *so much* they get obese in the process? A radioactive spill that shrivels all life in the area? Or best of all, *decomposing organisms coming back to life?*"

As he inched towards me, I stepped back hesitantly. "No,

Gilbert, it's just about how prehistoric animals' DNA was found and grown to make similar versions of the original creatures. Then, a lab mistake causes the creatures to be released earlier than expected, causing chaos and turmoil." His proud expression sulked slightly, and he said, "Not as menacing, but still in my league. What do you exactly need help with?"

"I don't know what words to add, substitute, or remove. Could you happen to educate me on that?"

Gilbert quickly skimmed through my essay and said, "Okay, maybe in your first paragraph, 'the saber-toothed cat pounces on the doctor and tears his human flesh with its long, razor-sharp teeth.'" "I think that's a *little* too gory."

Gilbert threw his hands in the air and said, "Well then, sorry dude, I usually write everything with macabre taste. So, I'm afraid I can't help you." He walked away without even acknowledging me. He then stopped and turned back to me. "Have you ever watched Jurassic Park?" he asked me. "No," I said.

"Why?" He replied, "If you're going to write this story, and I am going to help you, I'll be in serious trouble for plagiarism." I asked, "But why? I didn't copy this from anybody." He put a hand on my shoulder, and said, "Bro, just watch the movie." He walked off. Hmm. It was a catch-22. I'd have to change the story due to plagiarism, and I had to change it, anyhow, because I received no literary guidance.

I entered Livermore Middle School's gym, which seemed to be wider than Lake Tahoe itself. It was filled with symbols of the school mascot, Leo the Lion, grinning charmingly with the slogan, "Let's go, Lions!" I went to the changing room to put on my red and yellow jersey and shorts. When I came out, I jogged toward Coach Vencer, A.K.A. Vulture, and the rest of my classmates. He was a large man with a paunch and had a nefarious side smirk with his mouth half-open, which made me think he used to be (or still is) a cigar smoker. Everyone called him Vulture because he purposely put the weaker kids in PE with heftier kids, and after the weaker kids faced the unbearable, he would just say, “Well, you should’ve done more,” or “Come on, he didn’t hurt you *that* bad.” The problem was, even the principal couldn’t do anything about it, because the principal’s son was being engaged to Coach Vencer’s daughter, and he didn’t want to be the reason for his son’s break-up. Today, he told us, “Now, I would like to let you guys all in on a secret, something I believe to be very true. See, this is something you mainly use in a life-or-death situation, but still, it's very useful. Philosophy of school: Win by hook-or-crook. This doesn’t just apply to PE, my boys, but for even the tests and stuff. Whatever you gotta do, *just win*.” He smiled crookedly, then told us the rules of the game. “Whatever it takes,” he announced. “Whichever team has the most cones wins, and whichever team has the least,” he said bitterly, “Has to do fifty burpees before the bell rings.” The crowd "oo" ed at the severe penalty. "*Ready, steady,* RAID!" The kids were in a frenzy, pushing and shoving like Coach Vencer had implied to do. No matter what we did, our cones were stolen because the bigger kids pushed our barricade and stole our cones, and due to our team's lack of physical ability, we weren't able to make up for the cones stolen either. After the game, Vulture scowled at us and nodded to a corner. "Finish 'em up quickly; you only got a minute." I tried to do them quickly, which resulted in excessive perspiration and hyperventilation. *Note to self: Never end up in that situation again.*

Since my height was only 4'9", and I was in middle school, my dad would ask me to do extra physical activity, along with making me do height-increasing yoga, specific leg exercises designed for increasing height and building up strength in the leg muscles, and would do relaxing leg massages to my leg. Since all the effort went in vain, he would joke, "Nathan, you've increased one thousand nanometers!"

then laugh over it himself. A nanometer, of course, was one of the smallest units of measurement, and then came picometers, femtometers, and attometers. Thankfully, my school was very secure, and bullying happens very rarely, therefore proving that my height was perfectly *fine*. My dad would tell me, “I’m surprised I don’t see you beaten up after coming home. Hmm. Not like I *want* you to get beaten up, but still, height is important.” After the complaints of SpectersCloak23 and that incident with Danny, the school put tighter security in the school. I did feel insecure about my height from time to time, but then shrugged the feeling off. I just needed to go outside a little more and increase my calcium and protein intake, I guess. Vitamins, calcium, and protein are very important in growth.

I then suddenly sensed a message, probably to the coach.

Unknown User:

34-1-8 62-9-10 59-11-3 27-4-2 46-8-7

Judging by the amount of weird, unrelated numbers, I think that was a spam message. It has to be. Right?

I rang the doorbell to my house, and my mom opened the door. Noemi and I entered and saw a man sitting on our couch, chatting. He was wearing some sort of red-checkered turban, white robes, and a ring with a "*D*" branded on it. I wondered what it was supposed to signify, maybe his name? But something didn't feel right about it. I took my backpack off and freshened up. When the foreign man glanced at me, I had a feeling of hesitation creeping up my spine. He said, in his thick Arab accent, "Hello, young man." and smiled. My dad said to me, "It's time you meet one of my best buddies at college, Ibrahim Ayyad, but he is better known as Ibby." Ibby offered his hand, and reluctantly, I shook it. Dad might have told me about him, but I don't recollect why he mentioned him at that time. I sat and watched as they reminisced about their old times together. My mom came and offered him *chai* and some snacks. The discussion had skewed in many directions, from memories to asking about my siblings and me, and finally, the awkward questions and their answers that didn't trigger another topic. This usually happened at the end of anybody visiting, because the guest wanted to leave but didn't want to seem rude. So, the questions and their responses that went back and forth were blunt and straight-forward. They never exceeded four sentences. Then, they said their goodbyes and left. Somehow, my dad's friend felt threatening. As the posh Tesla left our driveway, I walked back inside, running upstairs to practice violin. A thought suddenly hit me. I needed to check Principal Davenport's messages. "*I'll do that first thing when I get to school tomorrow.*" I made a mental note.

Chapter 11

The Suspicious Letter "D"

"Nothing is hidden that will not be made known; nothing is secret that will not come to light."

– Dan Brown

When I got to school, everything was *so* different. The bullies I had suspended had returned, scanning the arriving students like hawks, trying to find even a clue of SpectersCloak23's identity. I shielded myself from their view by quickly taking a turn to the other hallway, towards the principal's office. And then what was even weirder, students taking these *orange pills* of some sort. When I took a closer look, the pills had the letter "D" imprinted on them, with the same exact font as the ring Ibby had. It couldn't be a coincidence. Somehow, Ibby was related to it all. I took a look at someone's pill bottle, and the prescription said the medication was Dexeplin. I should research this and find out more about it. I came to the door where clearly inscribed in bolded letters:

LLOYD DAVENPORT, PRINCIPAL

I put my ear to the door and waited for the messages to appear.

Kelly Robinson:

New announcement for all LVUSD academic staff:...

MAYBE- Janet Wallace:

Please come to our fundraising event here at Lorenzo Lutheran Church! We would greatly appreciate your presence!

Lloyd Davenport:

128-15-3 39-12-5 54-2-9 94-6-5 71- Owssrtl Oeeklpz, * o 97-5-10.

What is this *nonsense*? Was this based on a code of some sort? I believe these random numbers were similar to the ones I got from Coach Vencer's messages. And this Unknown User? Was this the same user from the hotel? The suspiciousness always leads to questions.

Unknown User:

201-16-7. 46-3-9 176-8-5.

I don't know what my principal got his hands into, but whatever it was, it *didn't* look good.

Crimson Comedor was a lavish restaurant with bright neon lights that blinded me. Tall tables were arranged neatly across the area, and a bar was placed in the corner. A mariachi band was there to entertain, and I found the style of the music very interesting. Tortilla chips straight out of the oven were brought to us, along with salsa and guacamole. Then the main dishes started coming in, filling up all the space on our table. Suddenly, I caught something in the corner of my eye. Sitting a few tables away from me was the unmistakable face… of *Ibrahim Ayyad*. He was wearing something similar to what he wore at my house, except royal blue. And sitting with him was my principal, Lloyd Davenport. This situation is becoming more suspicious by the minute. I was so stunned that Noemi had to come and snap in front of my eyes, chip crumbs flying everywhere. “What ya lookin’ at?” she said. She turned to where I was looking, and a matching expression took shape on her face. She whispered to me, “*You thinking what I’m thinking?*” I nodded, eyes wide. Well, I wasn’t thinking *exactly* what she was thinking, as I knew and sensed more than Noemi could comprehend. They seemed to be engaged in their conversation, with no sudden bursts of anger or laughter. After we finished eating, my dad also saw Ibby, and he walked over to him and said, “Hey, dude, how come you’re here?” When his eyes landed on the principal, his posture straightened, and he said, “Principal Davenport.” The principal looked at me and Noemi and recognized us as students in his middle school. Noemi glared at Ibby and the principal and asked, “*What are you two* doing?” She waved her fingers at both Ibby and the principal. Dad gave her a slight nudge and said, “Sorry, Principal, please don’t mind my daughter’s manners. How are they doing at school?” My dad was the concerned parent all of a sudden, and the principal replied, “Sir, I don’t have that information at the time. You should probably ask their teachers.”

A moment of silence passed, and finally, I spoke up. “Well, why are you two talking together? I wouldn’t think that you both would know each other.” Ibby looked at the principal and then said, “We met at a car sale in Germany, where I bought my Tesla,” he explained. “We became close friends after talking a lot about which cars we liked. And since then, we've been buddies." Whatever it was, I couldn't imagine my principal going to Germany to see cars. After all, he drives a 1995 Volkswagen Passat. He might have gone there to consider buying a new car. My dad glanced at his watch and said, "Well, it's getting late, and we need to go. Nice meeting you here. See you around, I guess." My mom pushed the door open, and then I caught a glimpse of the same D-branded ring on the principal's hand. It could have been a gift from Ibby, but it didn't appear so.

I stayed up a little late at night to research the drug I saw everyone using today. I had to dig, but I got a good chunk of the information I wanted. Dexeplin was a new medication launched into the market a few weeks ago for enhanced academic performance. That did explain why our classmates had begun to take pills. I found it odd that I didn't find any info about whether it was FDA-evaluated. How were the consumers of this medication so *careless*? This all sounded quite similar to the “supply” and “pharma” going on during Thanksgiving break. *The rings, the pills, the messages*. Everything had some indirect connection, but it was not so clear as to how. I did some comparisons to other drugs like fentanyl and methadone. My mom is in the biotech research field, so she knew quite a bit about medications and dosages. I asked her about it and added what she told me about it to my hippocampus(part of the brain responsible for memory, in simpler terms). The Dexeplin dosages weren’t as high as the ones in fentanyl and methadone, two main overdose-causing drugs. At least, the dosages are not as high… *yet*.

Chapter 12

Visit to the Temple

"Man is made by his beliefs. As he believes, so he is."

- Bhagavad Gita (17:3)

Today, my family was preparing to visit the most beautiful Hindu temple in the Bay Area, the Shiva-Vishnu temple. I had been there many times as a kid, where I used to run around from idol to idol and ask which God was which and what powers did they have. We hadn't visited in a long time, so we decided to pay a visit. We got up early in the morning, had a quick breakfast, brushed our teeth, and took a shower. We were ready so quickly that our hair was still damp. My dad and I wore a *kurta*, a long, thin, traditional shirt worn in South Asian culture. His was turmeric orange, and mine was cherry red. The ladies, though, had contrasting, cooler colors. Noemi and my mom wore the *lehenga choli*, another clothing worn by women in Indian and South Asian culture. My mom sported a majestic violet one and Noemi a turquoise *choli*. Usually, we would have an even amount of visits to the temple and the synagogue, which made us perfect Hin-Jews. One of the main reasons I liked the temple was the tranquility, the significance of each God and their story, and the priest's chanting and music. I had read many books about both of my religions, and Hinduism had many, many stories about each God. The main contrast between the two religions was Hindu polytheism versus Jewish monotheism. I respected the beliefs and teachings of both, but I wasn't aware if Noemi leaned towards one side. Temples generally had a main god or gods they were dedicated to, and this one was Shiva and Vishnu. These gods were part of the *Trimurti* or the three prevailing deities that are the primary forces of everything we know, existent and non-existent. We had *Brahma,* the creator, *Vishnu*, the preserver, and *Shiva*, the destroyer. They said that Vishnu and Shiva were both gods who listened to people's thoughts and cravings in a trance or meditation. This is why I could relate to these gods because I could intercept messages, which were basically the modern world's thoughts and feelings. There were many other gods that would be in the temple and idols or images representing them. So far, I hadn't experienced much messaging going on in the temple, nor had I in the synagogue. People tend to focus a lot on religion. When we were on the way to the temple, we would always listen to music albums of sacred Hindu chants in the car. All were very musical and pleasant to hear and involved the detailed pronunciation of Sanskrit phrases. As we listened deeply to the calming hymns, we had a sudden halt to our car's steady driving. Oh, *no*. This *couldn't* be happening. Not right now! My dad got out of the car, and took a look at the tires, then opened the hood to see what was wrong. He waved a hand to ward off the pungent, black smoke emitting from the car. He closed the hood, came back, and sighed. "Well, guys, whether you like it or not, the alternator fried. We're gonna have to *push*." We all groaned and got out of the car. We slammed the door, and I felt pity for the poor car. We shook our arms, then propelled the car forward at a snail's pace with our poor strength. After a long time, we finally managed to get it into a nearby parking lot. My father pulled out his phone and said, "It says we're about two miles from the temple. Phew. So, it'll take about thirty to forty-five minutes." Noemi whined with despair. "So let's walk fast." My dad declared, determined.

After we walked halfway, our posture skulking in exhaustion, a red Subaru pulled up beside us. I recognized who it was immediately. The front door's window opened. "Hey, Sofia," Ethan's mom said. Ethan waved from the front seat in a T-shirt and shorts. I waved back. "Why are you guys walking?" she inquired. "Oh, thank God you guys came." It was kind of ironic, as we *were* going to a religious place of worship. "Something burned in our car, and we were heading to the temple. Could you please drop us there?" my mom desperately pleaded. "Sure, sure, I was just heading nearby to drop Ethan off at his tennis classes." Of course, their family was forever indebted to mine for stopping Ethan's gaming addiction and raising his grades, but I didn't like to think that way. I didn't believe that family or friends should owe each other for doing favors for one another unless that person or those persons were too demanding or ignorant of others' convenience. "Thank you all so much." my mom restated on behalf of our entire family. Then she glared at us viciously for not expressing our gratitude. We mouthed "sorry" to her. We then were once again transported in a car, a much more efficient and quicker way to travel. It was a lucky coincidence that that happened. Soon enough, we were right in front of a white temple with a large pyramid-like structure in the middle. Most temples I have been to were architecturally symmetrical, like this one. The temple had a South Indian structure style. As we entered, we were filled with the deep sound of spiritual chants. We put our shoes on a shoe rack, as we weren't allowed to enter the worship center with shoes on. Taking off your shoes in the temple showed respect to the gods and kept the temple with its holy and clean vibe. We entered the worship center, stood before each idol, and prayed. My dad had given Noemi and me some short prayers dedicated to each God when we were young, so we recited those after visiting them. After offering obeisances to most of the idols, we headed over to get *Prasad*. *Prasad* was food given to people by the temple after offering it to a deity. The type of *Prasad* varied, from almonds and bananas to sweets such as *halwa* and *laddus*. Today, since there wasn't any special Hindu holiday or event, the *Prasad* was very simple. There were three priests, or *pujaris*, distributing the *prasad* to the people standing in line. When it was our turn, we each got a banana and two almonds. When we reached the third priest, he poured a drop of holy water from his metal tumbler into our hand. We drank it. This water, or *theertham*, is holy water given to one by the *pujaris* to purify oneself. I think to add the taste of the water, they put cardamom, cloves, and other spices. I could never tell, but my mom could. The days we got some tasty, mouth-watering sweets were the major events in the temple, with lots of crowds and queues to get to see the idols and get *Prasad*. Afterward, we went to see a few more statues and prayed, then went to retrieve our shoes. There had once been a time when we had lost our shoes in the temple because there were at least one thousand devotees that had visited the temple that day. It was *Shivrathri*, a festival dedicated to *Shiva*, and many people had dumped their shoes in one big pile on our shoes. We spent at least half an hour searching for them, but we simply couldn't find them. My mom gave up in the first ten minutes, my dad five minutes after her. Noemi and I were relentlessly persistent like the CIA finding a criminal. My mom practically had to drag us away from the temple. "You can check tomorrow. I one hundred percent guarantee it will be there." I remember my dad said as we drove back home that day, socks only. And lo, the next day, all of our shoes nicely huddled together in the rack. It made us omit the whole incident from our memory. After that, though, we were more careful about where we put our shoes. At least that day, we got succulent *Prasad*. It made up for the incident.

Chapter 13

Burnt Dessert, Brilliant Idea

"The only way you improve is to try new things."
– Charles Koch

Today at school, I had a quiz to do about major people in the Industrial Revolution. I also had a science test, and my final draft was due. I prayed for good grades. At least it wasn't as bad as Bill, whose average grade in almost everything is in the 30s. Mine were from ninety to one hundred, which are all A's.

When I got back from school, the smell of burnt dessert filled the house. Noemi yelled, "Dad, did you do one of your *experiments*?" My dad always liked to test out different things in the kitchen. The result usually ended up too burnt, bitter, spicy, etc. We didn't normally waste food, so we *had* to eat it. I know, fate, so cruel, indeed. When I walked into the kitchen, he jabbed his fork in and took a bite of his newest creation, which looked like a completely roasted marzipan. When he chewed for a while, his eyebrows shot up in surprise. He announced aloud, “Success! This is *really* good!” Noemi, not accepting the fact at first, put a piece in her mouth. She also was astonished, then satisfied. While munching on the marzipan, she nodded her head. “Somehow, you’re right this time, Dad. It’s amazing.” I, not wanting to miss out, took a slice and stuffed it in my mouth. The warm dessert was incredibly delicious, the tangy-tasting substance melting in my mouth. My saliva shot out like a jacuzzi, fuzzy bread massaging my palate. It was like I was in seventh heaven, a state of ecstatic bliss. I wished I could drink a whole ocean of lemon goo. The food made me feel gluttonous like I could eat it for eternity. I nodded my head rapidly in agreement. “It somehow makes you crave for it.” Noemi blurted out. My dad’s smile was so big it was touching his ears. He finally said, “Go freshen up. You guys just came from school, and you haven’t even set down your backpacks. That is the greatness of my delicacies!” Noemi started clapping sarcastically, shaping what you’d call an “I’ve-heard-this-a-million-times-and-I’m-so-bored” look. I intervened and said, “Come on, he has a point. This was his first best creation yet!” Dad pointed his finger at me and nodded as if to indicate, “Of course.” but then looked back in surprise at “first best creation yet.” Noemi mumbled, “Yeah, whatever.” and went to unpack, and I joined her soon after.

The main discussion during dinner was about the tongue-tingling dessert that Dad made. I stayed out of it. The thought of interfering and the whole family raising their voices to drown out the others, sheesh, no way. Instead, I thought about that day in history when I learned about the long-distance communication known as "Morse code." "*Can I somehow enhance my ability? How?*" were the questions ringing in my mind. I quietly finished the kurma, an Indian dish my dad was quite fond of, washed my plate, and set it gently in the dish drying rack. From the kitchen window, in the distance, I saw the cell tower standing tall in the sky, its wires intertwining and connecting cities. That was when an idea popped up. Cell phone towers. That's the key! By using cell towers to get messages out of my range, I could read and process messages more and solve this mystery! But how could I prove it? I'd have to test it out myself. Testing starts tomorrow! It looks like by sampling over-cooked but amazingly delicious dessert. I may just have to sample a brilliant idea. Inspiration comes from irrelevant things, I suppose.

Chapter 14

Training is Straining

"A new idea must not be judged by its immediate results."

– Nikola Tesla

School was pleasant because when I entered my classroom, everyone was eyeing my desk. When I went to see what was going on, I saw all the papers face-up with a "100!!" on my desk. Topping the class is definitely pleasant. Obviously, there were other individuals, Ernest, for example, who would, no matter what, pass. But still, I need to keep my "image" maintained. I shot everyone a sly grin, sat down in my seat, and waited for Mr. Volkov as he finished his discussion with the other teachers. There wouldn't be much today, just a few warm-ups for reviewing previous topics before starting the new one. There was a science presentation I had to do, though, but I was well prepared for it. I wouldn't have to fret over it. I'll get a lot of time today in school and unhurriedly wait for it to end. Then, enhancement practice will start. After finishing the first three periods of the day, I entered Mr. Nuñez's room. His classroom was a fairly short but wide room, with science posters on every wall or cabinet. It was dimly lit most of the time, as Mr. Nuñez was a science teacher who took energy conservation seriously. There was a large yellow fountain near the entrance for washing harmful chemicals out of the eyes, and he had many other types of science equipment as well. "Good morning, class; how has your day been going?" the teacher started off. "Are we all prepared for our presentations?" The class nodded. He smiled, went to organize some papers at his desk, and started typing on his keyboard. Since we had some time before class started, I skimmed through what I would be saying in my presentation. After some time, Mr. Nuñez rose from his seat and said, “All rightie, who’s up?” Many people raised their hands, but I didn’t. I wanted to appear after a few people did their turns. If I started, I would appear too over-confident and pompous. After the first few presentations and twenty minutes of class had gone by, I raised my hand. “Nathan, please enter the stage!” Mr. Nuñez said encouragingly. I walked up with a professional attitude and began my presentation. I didn’t use a very formal level of English and spoke semi-formally, so I would seem top-notch to the audience. The presentation was about showing people the negative effects of a bad habit(which the presenter selected) on each body system that we learned. After I had hooked my audience’s attention with an intro, I proceeded to explain the bad effects of a drug overdose on the circulatory system. After finishing that system and the respiratory, I continued on to the last body system discussed in class. “And now, the digestive system…” I announced and released some gas from behind. After the class heard what

I said and did, they snickered at the irony and pinched their nose in disgust. Even though I found it slightly amusing as well, I couldn't hide the blush I had gotten from the embarrassment. "Hey, a person farts about thirteen to twenty-one times a day. So, don't blame me." I finished up my presentation a little bit after, thankfully, without any other gaseous interruptions. "Let's all give a round of applause for Nathan." Mr. Nuñez announced. The class clapped so loudly that I was afraid the windows would start to break. *See*, I told myself. *A bit of accidental humor doesn't hurt.*

After some self-realization, I found out that my capability range was very poor. At maximum, I could rate myself a 3G. In the evening, I asked my mom if I could play outside for some time, and she allowed me. Excellent. She had just begun to prepare dinner for the family, and she wasn't looking at her phone. It was lying unattended on the sofa, and I could freely slip it into my pocket without anyone noticing. I opened the door to my backyard, and a pungent motor smell entered the house. A roaring sound droned on loudly in my ears, and I realized that the lawn mower was on. Great. I shut the door and walked towards the entry of the house. I clicked open the latch and unlocked it. The grass was newly trimmed, and the trees swayed serenely in the wind. I marched down the walkway to my house and cut across the front yard. I set the phone on a nearby tree branch and ran across to the other side of the house. What I was aiming to do was to keep the device that would receive the text messages slightly farther than what is usually my maximum sensing capabilities. Then, I would try to split my focus between the device that would receive the messages and the cell tower. I didn't know if it would do anything, but it was worth a shot. I was trying to harness the range distribution of the cell tower and apply that energy to the receiving device. It sounds like I just formulated this from half-baked scientific theories, but I did some research about all of this. I concentrated on the cell tower and felt some sort of brain "pull."

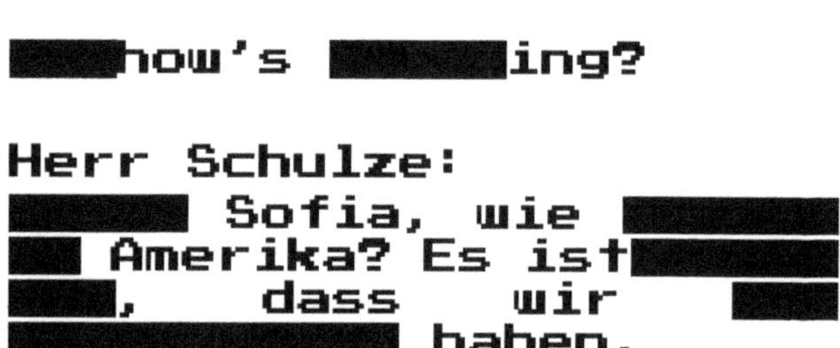

The concentration needed was so large that my temple started to throb loudly. My ears began to ring, and I couldn't move a muscle. Tears formed in my eyes, and beads of sweat dropped down as I surged in pain. I sucked in a deep breath and let it out erratically. Even if I put this much energy into getting the messages, they wouldn't even come clearly. Sighing with relief, I limped towards the tree branch where I had left the phone. I heard a large "thud" and a "crack," and when I looked up at the branch, nothing was there. I looked down and saw the phone. I picked it up and stared at the screen in horror. The screen was cracked. It must have fallen on a stone or something. Oh, *fish*. My mom will *kill* me. I carefully put the fragile item in my pocket and went back inside. Then I tiptoed my way across to the sofa before anybody noticed me, and I slid the phone under it. Phew. I'm saved from punishment. They'll just assume it fell(which it did, but under my watch). Hopefully.

Chapter 15

36 Hours of Peace

"Sometimes the best lighting of all is a power failure."

– Douglas Coupland

Today, along with all the other days this occurred, was one of the best days of the year. The electricity went out because of a power outage, and in recent years, it has been happening a lot. Since every day, without fail, messages would flood my skull, today, nothing. Absolute peace, relief, solace, ultimate tranquility. In fact, I let this bliss get to my head as I was skipping around the house, careful not to bump into anything in the darkness. My mom asked, with an eyebrow raised, "What happened to you, Nathan? You look *so* happy today!?" I hugged my mom and said, "Well, it's fun in this darkness.

Feels like we're camping in a cave or something." Of course, the *main* reason wasn't that, but I had to say something. The school was canceled today, and since all of our assignments are online nowadays, we couldn't even complete our homework, so I had free time in the house. I would have used my time to exercise my powers, but since there was a power outage, I decided to devote that time to helping my parents do the household jobs. As I quickly finished washing the dishes and taking out the trash, my mom thanked me by saying, "You're so kind and helpful, mein Liebling. Of course, you're my son, so why wouldn't you be kind and helpful?" The sun was setting, illuminating the sky with an orange glow. I put the dishes on the table for dinner, and now, since the sunlight was gone, we had a candlelight dinner. We talked about our safety because of the earthquakes nearby, causing the blackout. We had a shelter in place, but my dad said that the extremity of the earthquakes is yet to be determined. The candle's light flickered erratically, then extinguished itself, leaving the burnt smell of lavender-scented candles. My mom rushed to get the matchbox, and we resumed eating afterward. So far, I was enjoying this! I soon went to sleep after we played a game of Uno, Crazy 8's, and Monopoly. If it continued like this, I would be living a peaceful yet poorly lit life. The next day also went like this, with the family having a day of fun without electronics until…

The lights flickered on. We had to take a second to adjust to the sudden light in the house. The TV turned on, a news anchor blaring about the recent earthquakes. Uh-oh. This was the part I *hated* the most. The *overload*. I was thrown back, a flood of messages piling up inside me, the pressure tough to withstand. The longer the blackout, the more messages would come. Why couldn't people just wait to send things for *one* day? Why couldn't they just *take a break* and chill during the blackout? My parents shielded my eyes. Poor things; they always thought that I was photosensitive after the "overload" used to occur when I first developed my power. They also thought it had something to do with my weird need for glasses with electronic devices. Since then, they've been careful about letting me see too many action movies. I always shrugged them off when the light-flickering scenes would occur, and they've always wondered why it happened after blackouts specifically. But they started to live with it, and it hasn't been a problem. "Here you go, bud, some water." my dad said as he handed me a glass. I drank it, and I sighed. Messages, online homework, and more messages. Looks like my peacetime is over.

Chapter 16

Lost & Found

"When twins are separated, their spirits steal away to find the other."

- Jandy Nelson

Most people from my elementary school knew Larry and Ferry, the inseparable, identical twins. Larry and Ferry could only be told apart by their walking style. Larry would walk with one shoulder slightly raised than the other; his body tilted so his lower shoulder was in front. He dragged his back foot, and this all made him seem like a hooligan or gangster of some kind. Ferry walked upright and formally, which displayed his more mature nature, which was the physical and behavioral feature that kept the brothers discernable. We would always keep a distance from them, then ask them to come over to where we were so we could tell who's who(it would be embarrassing to keep asking them their name instead). Unfortunately, today, Larry went missing, and it was becoming very common to see "MISSING KID" signs pasted everywhere. Of course, nobody seemed to care, and the signs didn't make much of a difference(which made it a waste of paper, too). We tried to inform everybody in the neighborhood and school to contact us if they found him. According to all the crime movies I've seen, the first forty-eight hours were crucial for people who went missing. After that, the police didn't really look into it much, and they assumed the individual was dead. We still had hope that Lawrence "Larry" Archer was still out there. I realized that my ability could help solve this problem. So, I dedicated my day to my third hemisphere, tuning in to any suspicious activity or clue regarding Larry's disappearance. Later that evening, my mom took me to a local Albertson's to get my mind off of the ordeal. We would have completely been in oblivion to it if I hadn't gotten the message:

Ferry:

Sorry, L. I messed up. I shouldn't have run.

Holy identity mix-up! It wasn't Larry, but Ferry! I knew he had to be somewhere nearby, but I would have immediately spotted him if he had been inside the store. I told my mom, "Mom, my friends got new news. Ferry is the one missing, not Larry. They tracked his location and found him somewhere around here. I told them I was going to Albertson's today, which is nearby. If you could allow me to search for him, please?" My mom couldn't deny this request. It was about a missing child, after all. She quickly ran a marathon across the entire store, added all the things she needed to the cart, and rushed to retrieve Ferry. We put our groceries in the trunk and then circled the perimeter of Albertson's. That's when we saw a small campfire in the distance behind the store. “Ferry!” I shouted as I ran over to inspect the fire. There he was, the auburn hair and eyes glinting like sapphire gems in the light. He sat on a stone, his posture sunken in sadness. I didn’t know what to say. I mean, if you find one of your friends after they went missing, and you realize that they weren’t even the friend you thought you were looking for, and it was that friend’s twin brother, then I didn’t think that a “Hi, how are you doing?” was a good start to the conversation.

“*Oh, hi, Nathan*,” he mumbled, soon catching my presence.

“What happened? Everybody’s been searching everywhere for you!” I exclaimed, concerned.

“Eh, I didn’t think I would find you here, but this was because I was having a hard time at home, and I needed a break. I think I should be heading back.”

“If you want, you could hitch a ride back home with us?” I offered.

He shrugged. “Okay, sure. Thank you, Nathan.” Ferry and I sat in the back seats, and my mom drove Ferry to his apartment complex. He thanked us once again and proceeded towards his home. Well, it certainly was a supercalifragilisticexpialidocious day. Now I could tell the tale of how I saved the Archer twins, Lawrence and Ferdinand, Larry and Ferry, Lost and Found. Of course, I *wouldn't* tell the tale because then my third hemisphere secret would be out. No, no, no, this tale is for me to keep.

Chapter 17

Training Gets Delayed

"Ideas without action are useless."

– Helen Keller

2 DAYS LATER
DECEMBER 2, 2018

My training has slumped behind because I didn't want to risk losing another phone. Noemi was hunting down every possible suspect in what she called "The Phone Mystery." She dressed up in her obnoxious Sherlock Holmes costume as she examined each and every note on the bulletin board with a magnifying glass. Her notes were so detailed that I feared she would catch me soon enough. Drained, I decided to laze around on the same nightmare-giving couch. I had nothing to do today; it was a weekend, and I completed my homework early. I could lie around all I wanted. I felt like a balloon, the helium all gone and plastic scraps remaining. Exhaustion turned to drowsiness, and drowsiness turned to dormancy. Half an hour later, my dad rested a hand on my shoulder and gently whispered, “Nathan, wake up, bud. It’s time for lunch.” I popped my eyes open and blinked. I sat up straight and tried to regain my alertness. I walked to the dining room, and I saw a porcelain bowl with salad in it. Noemi helped Mom pass out the dishes while I just sat down in my seat, my laziness at its highest. I served myself some salad and gripped my fork and knife. As I started to grind the veggies between my teeth, I thought, “*Maybe I shouldn’t test my ability at home. It’ll be risky, but I’ll need a friend to help me.*” Who should I ask? Half of them would think I’m crazy and shoo me away, and part of them would snatch that idea for a sci-fi essay. Someone like Ernest, probably. He sided well with me during our “bully-hunting” days. Yup, Ernest, it is. To be honest, I was kind of getting tired of calling him 'Ernest.' I'll ask him if I can call him something simpler, like 'Ernie.' I hoped I wouldn't come across as rude and he wouldn't help with my training. So I suppose I probably *shouldn't* do that.

"Good news," said my dad. "I just received a promotion, and I want to celebrate. We're gonna fill our tummies with Coke and popcorn and watch a movie in a drive-in theater!" The announcement was met by a jubilant round of applause. "Not *too* much, though," warned Mom. "Two Cokes max."

We were seated atop our car, the orange sunset illuminating the sky. In big, red letters, the screen read, "*Free Guy*, STARTS IN 2 MINUTES." Dad and Noemi were already crunching on the popcorn and sipping *Coca-Colas*. My family is known for being updated on new releases because, as per the messages I can sense from my parents' phones, everyone in the neighborhood asked my parents about the new movies. They usually had trouble remembering the names of the movies, and then I would have to remind them. This also had to do with my power. I could sense messages relating to the release of new movies. For example, I once told my mom, "You know, the new Marvel movie is coming soon, *Infinity War*. We should go to the theater for that."

My mom had said, "How do you get all this movie info?"

"Research." I would say, as a substitute for "Mental power which lets me read text messages."

My mom probably remembered every German movie she had watched back in the day. My dad only remembered the iconic Hindi movies of his time and would whistle some tunes or say some famous dialogues from them. I remembered many of the movies I had seen, although I assumed this wasn't a genetic thing. Whenever there was a remake of a movie, I would recognize it almost immediately and alert the family. They always were amazed at my memory. Of course, I didn't only try to remember the names of movies. It just came naturally. I focused on remembering important facts about the world, current events and hot topics, and things that would make me seem intelligent so I could fit in a crowd of adults.

The family would mainly watch English movies but sometimes explore movies in our own languages like German and Hindi. Of course, since I wasn't very fluent in either, subtitles were needed from time to time. I knew I was close to learning both languages. Watching movies in other languages somehow increased my bilingual vocabulary. I wasn't able to increase my knowledge of Hindi and German because we didn't watch movies in those languages very frequently. I would have to ask my parents to change that.

Mom mumbled to me, "Nathan, I like these moments when the family spends time together, don't you?" I regarded the statement by nodding affectionately towards my mother.

She hugged me, and we waited as the countdown for the movie began. After the movie, we went to a nearby restaurant and had dinner. I didn't think this was the best way to celebrate Dad's promotion, but it was still okay. We got in the car, and the car started with a high-pitched beep and a guttural grunt of objection. The time read 9:34, which meant that we needed to get home and go directly to bed; otherwise, Mom wouldn't be so happy about it. But I couldn't sleep, the mere thought of being able to sense messages more than I was ever capable of.

The next day, after school, my training got delayed even more. My dad, the typical "middle-aged gardening guy," invited me to come along with him on his coffee runs. Coffee runs, a tradition started when I was nine, was a technique he found to help his crops thrive. Coffee grounds are rich in nitrogen, which stimulates the growth of plants. Every once or twice a month, my dad and I went to a local Starbucks and asked around for this agricultural coffee. Some of the stores were very plentiful and gave us a fair amount of coffee, while others were ignorant and claimed that they "didn't have it." It was not fair. The plants get coffee every month, and I get it every year! Human rights, people. But I shouldn't feel greedy. Drinking coffee is a temporary enjoyment, and it will leave as soon as the coffee cup is finished.

My backyard was a peaceful, calm haven to walk away from your troubles. It was one of the things I liked the most about my house. There was a flower garden with roses, magnolias, tulips, and many other different types of flowers. Alongside that was a vegetable garden, where we grew bell peppers, eggplants, cucumbers, okra, and varieties of other veggies needed for my mom's cooking. My dad was in control of this area, and in his free time, he would tend to the plants like they were his own children. Sometimes, my mom, Noemi, and I would help him set up a garden bed or plant seeds with him. There was an area next to the garden where our pool was, although it wasn't too big. Small river rocks with unique colors and shapes acted as a border between the pool area and the garden. Very close to the border was a large population of mint that thrived like a metropolis, and every so often, we would have to cut the mint until only one stem was left. Since its growth properties were similar to that of weeds, the mint jungle would grow back within a span of a week. My dad didn't know that it would grow to such an extent when he planted it. In the corner of the backyard in the pool area, a big Buddha statue sat in its meditating pose underneath the shade of a tree in the woods behind my house. This was a factor in creating the relaxing, tranquil vibe of my backyard.

As I sat waiting in the car, I heard the car beep. As the trunk opened, my dad said, "Forty pounds from this one. How many do we have so far?" We measured not by how many bags of coffee but by how much it *weighed*. I sighed, then did the addition in my head. "*30+25+40=95*." "Ninety-five pounds," I said. "Do you wanna break our streak of 155 pounds?" my dad asked, trying to coax me. If I agreed, then we would probably have to go to ten different Starbucks', and only a few of which were in Livermore. If it risked going to a nearby town, making it late for dinner, and getting some awful scoldings from Mom, *then no*. "Well, Dad, it's already 7:30, and we shouldn't make it late for dinner." I half-pleaded. My dad shrugged and then started the car. "To home," he proclaimed, then muttered, "*Of course, Nathan is right. Nobody in the entire world wants Sofia screaming. Nobody*." That was what you called a "tiger mom." A mother that strikes fear in the hearts of her family. It's a pretty dramatic title, I do admit.

Chapter 18

Goodbye, Morty

"The comfort of having a friend may be taken away, but not that of having had one."

- Seneca

I had a friend in my physical education and Spanish classes, Morty, a chubby blond who wore different colored Crocs to school every day. Since we saw each other in two consecutive classes and we shared a similar end-of-day biking route, we were pretty good buddies. He was very timid, helping everybody around him, and wasn't the one to say bad words or break rules. He would be picked on frequently, but since Ernest and I had curbed bullying in school, he had been feeling more confident in school. He was amongst the general population of kids with low grades, and his parents had decided to try out the orange, D-branded focus pills for performance enhancement and the capability to study for hours. The sudden increase in study time had given Morty bags under his eyes, as well as glasses, which didn't suit his plump physique. His glasses had different colors in a tortoiseshell kind of pattern on their frame, and he alternated his croc colors based on it. Morty's father, Mr. Michael Epstein, a hefty middle-aged man, worked as a salesman, and Mrs. Matilda Epstein, a graceful orange-haired lady, was a receptionist at a hotel. They were very concerned about their son's progress, so they resorted to taking the Dexeplin pills as part of a daily prescription. The nurse would come down to Morty's classroom and give him a pill once in the afternoon after lunch. Of course, he had his own stock at home from which he would take his meds. It was all going well; Morty's grades were going up, and his confidence and performance changed drastically(but in a good way). Until one day, Morty came to school with a very bubbly, hyperactive mood. He started to talk faster, his leg began to quiver often, he started to exert more energy and do more physical activity in PE, and he finished quizzes and exit tickets with such rapid pace and accuracy. I mean, doing more physical activity and finishing assignments fast wasn't that big of a deal, but the change in behavior, attitude, and speech. *This* was not the Morty I knew. Deep down, I knew this was because of his meds. Everybody thought they were helping him, but maybe they were just making him *worse*.

After Morty's grades began to finally settle in the passing A-B zone, his parents began to take him off of his medication. But that just made him more awful. What resulted was terrible mood swings and drowsiness, and his improving grades plummeted like an asteroid. I felt sorry for him and wished he got better. Unfortunately, he had gotten hooked on the orange poison disguised as medicine. It had plagued his mind; it was an addiction. I had initially expected the dreadful, unfortunate day to go normal. But what I saw was people standing next to a small framed photo of Morty, with the words;

In remembrance of our dearly departed friend, Morton Epstein

Candles were gathered around the photo, and many students set roses to mourn the death of Morty. Morty smiled gleefully in his picture, his teeth out, dimples in his blubber-like, rosy cheeks. The sea-green eyes that once sparkled with life and excitement are now gone. His mother stood in a corner, sniffling into a tissue. “It was all going normal,” she squeaked. “And then he started having a seizure. That was unusual since no previous problems like that had occurred, and no genetic history showed any chance of that happening. We rushed him to the hospital, and…” She burst out into an emotional fit. “*He didn’t make it.*”

All the teachers who knew Morty as a well-behaved kid who had just improved his grades sobbed. My eyes welled up with tears, but I held them back. What was supposed to be done wasn't to cry, but to learn from his situation. Innocent people like Morty, who relied on pills to take care of their grades or help them focus in school but then got addicted and died, that wasn't gonna happen. Not on my watch. I would ensure that.

Nobody seemed to realize how the drugs were affecting Morty. They all just thought it was a simple accident. Despite the amount of times our counselors have ranted about the use of legal drugs and addiction, the message wasn't being passed. I'd have to find out more about what secrets the Dexeplin pills were hiding. What exactly had happened to Morty? Was he taking his medications improperly, or was he following the dosage *correctly*, but the amount of the drug was not as it was on the label? These questions swirled through my mind like a violent hurricane. I would make sure that this hurricane does some damage before settling. My questions *deserved* answers. This incident will forever be chiseled in my memory, not to simply remember, but to *fight*.

At the end of the day, I was exiting the building through the gym when I saw some people cleaning out Morty's locker. Along with his gym clothes and sports shoes, there was a pill container with some pills remaining. They set his things in a tray for the custodians to clean up, and a little while after they left, I snuck his pill bottle into my pocket and went to the bus stand. I needed to get this tested so my doubts would be answered. I must get an important understanding of what was going on with Dexeplin before I would carry out a mission with no aim. Finding out the issue was of top priority right now, so I can avenge accordingly. Now, I not only needed Ernest to help me expand the range of my sixth sense, but I also needed him to help me get to the bottom of what illicit secrets the Dexeplin pills were hiding.

Chapter 19

Revealing Causes Disappointment

"A true friend is someone you can trust with all your secrets."

– Unknown

The next day, before the first period, I walked over to Ernest. I said, "Hey, haven't talked to you in a while." He mumbled, "Same here," while gathering his materials. He closed his locker and finally looked up at me. "Actually, I wanted…" we said in sync. Well, great minds think alike, I suppose. I said politely, "You can go ahead." He said, "Okay, I understand how you got the information about Danny and his stealing plan, but for the rest of the bullies, how did you know when they were going to strike?" I whispered, "I also wanted to talk to you about something along those lines." The first-period bell hollered resoundingly, interrupting our conversation. "Meet after school?" I offered. Ernest gave me a thumbs-up, and I headed for history class.

At Ernest's house, I sat in silence, waiting for Ernest to wrap his head around what I said. "Wait a minute, you're telling me that you have some sort of 'WhatsApp brain,' and you have an ability related to snooping on other people's messages?!"

I sighed. "Ernest, I've said 'yes,' like, fifty-three times or something. I have better things to do." I pointed out. "And no, I don't voluntarily snoop on people's text messages. It just happens."

"If what you're saying is true, and I don't *completely* believe it's true, then show me," Ernest demanded. "*Fine*," I grumbled. I waited, eyes closed, waiting for any message to flicker into view.

Britannica:

New Article: Elections in the U.S. Since The 17th Century

"You just got a new article from Britannica about U.S. elections," I said. Ernest looked at his phone, and his mouth dropped open. But his amazed expression slowly twinged with betrayal. I was puzzled to see this sudden change in expression. "You know, Nathan, I befriended you because I was always left out. Some of the friends I had deserted me because I was over-honest and always blurted out their secrets. Their secrets were of no value, and it didn't hurt anyone to learn some truths. I respect the truth, and I know that sometimes, the truth needs to be kept confidential. *You* were the only one that saw that in me, Nathan. Yet you kept a secret like that from your friend. Your friend, Nathan, not anybody else. *How could you?*"

I was appalled by the statements, like bullets shot from a pistol. "No, but Ernest… you said that sometimes the truth needs to be hidden. I haven't even told my parents!" I did have a point. There was a slight sense of hypocrisy in what Ernest was saying. "Don't talk to me, Nathan," he said coldly. I could see his emotions were mixing in his head. Anger, sorrow, shock. They were swirling in one giant tornado within him, and I knew the feeling. At some point, he would either "shatter" with sadness, "erupt" with fury, or settle down. But I could tell he knew the feeling, too, and before he caused any damage, he left the room in a huff. I took it as a cue to leave and decided to give him a few days to forgive me. Finally, two days after I revealed my condition to Ernest, he asked me, "So, why did you choose to tell me your secret? What good will I do?"

"I need a reliable buddy to help me enhance and train the extent of my power. There is an ulterior motive to this, which you'll know when you help me. Can I trust you?" I said, and then I offered my hand. He stared at my gesture, considering the recent fallout we both had. After some thought, he shook my hand. “When shall we start the training? Next Thursday works for me.” Ernest informed me. I was relieved to see him back to his normal, sane, smart attitude. “Next Thursday it is.” I declared.

“Listen, Nathan, your mom and I have been discussing…” my dad said to me. I rolled my eyes. “Dad, is it about p-”

“None of the sort, son. We were discussing you taking summer classes.” my mom said enthusiastically. I shrugged and mumbled, “Sure. What classes are they?” “Tennis and taekwondo lessons. The good part about tennis is it’s not a team sport, so you aren’t left out of a game. Equal contribution. And taekwondo will help improve your strength and agility,” my dad added factually. Like *I* wasn’t strong enough or didn’t have good stamina. *Whatever*.

I suppose it's for my benefit. It could even improve the way I am able to sense messages. You never know until you try, right?

“Is Noemi coming with me?” I asked. They nodded. I then said, “Good, I'll have some extra activity to look forward to.” There was a sudden moment of silence. My mom broke the tension by saying, “I'm heading to the kitchen to make pasta. Nathan, pass out the dishes.” I regarded my mom with a small thumbs-up and headed to do the necessary.

On Thursday, I told Ernest about the hotel incident and how it seemed to be like something suspicious was trending. He pointed out that we should work together to get some clues. We split the teamwork: I did the “online sensory” stuff, and he did the detective work. He brought me to the school's soccer field after school, which was good because there was a cell tower nearby. Ernest squatted down and rested his hands on his thighs. He said, “Okay, um, I guess, you know… just do your thing. Sorry, I don’t know how to put it.” I gave him a “it’s okay” gesture and began to try it out. Ernest had put his phone on the other side of the field just to strain the distance. I began, hands floating at my sides, my mind one with the cell tower, sensing Ernest’s messages.

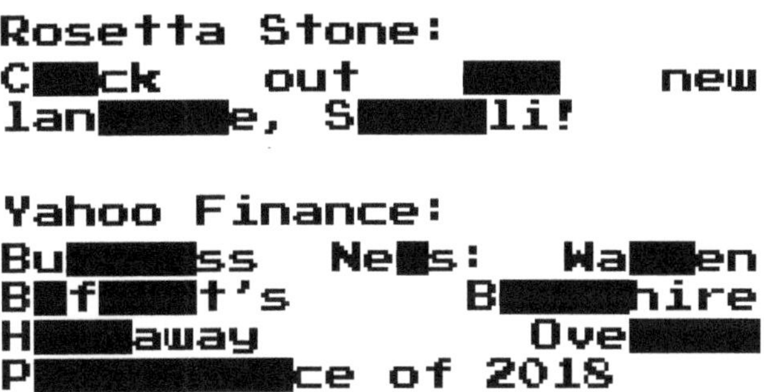

Again, the pressure was tough to withstand, the mind tug extreme. My face cringed in concentration, and my ears rang deafeningly. I released the pressure and gasped for breath. I croaked out, “*Water. Need water.*” Ernest acted quickly, heaving my weight up on his shoulder and guiding me to the water fountain. I didn’t care where the water landed, as any form of hydration seemed to be the most refreshing thing in the world.

Afterward, when I came home all sweaty, my dad said, “Looks like you drenched yourself. What game did you play?” I stammered. “Yes, er…um, soccer, that is. It was a tough game.” My dad nodded, then said, “Go take a shower. You probably would need that.” I certainly agreed. After some strong third-hemisphere training, showers were one of the best remedies to cool down.

I recently bought some books from Costco about brain-training exercises in an attempt to strengthen my skills. After Ernest had recorded my recent message interceptions, I *don’t* think it had made much use. It was fun, though. I enjoyed my time completing the puzzles in *Big Word Puzzles*, *501 Puzzles to Keep Your Brain Young*, and *Left and Right Brain Training*.

Ernest and I had timed ourselves on many of these activities. Ernest had won most of them, however, increasing our competition. But of course, Ernest was a word whiz, a math master, and a tech expert. So, there *really* was no point in competing with a genius like him. We also tried to improve the use of our non-dominant hands. I was right-handed, Ernest was left-handed, and so it made it fun where we would tease each other for not being able to write on each other's strong hand. Ernest, the scientist, thought that if I could sharpen the other skill sets of my brain, then my message radar would increase its radius. Ernest wrote all of his findings and theories on my power in a Google Doc and titled it "NathanBauer_CaseStudy." The title kind of made me feel like I was being experimented on, but it's fine. He wrote all the messages I intercepted in a small pocket-sized journal. This was always useful because if I had found any suspicious messages related to the ones I intercepted at the hotel or anything in general that we were capable of solving.

I had a specific method of learning things and grasping them, and it reflected my determination. I assumed expanding and learning more about my ability would follow the same steps. This technique would be the way I could have a larger message interception radius after training and solve the mysterious events happening around Livermore. The best example of this in my past was how I learned to ride a bike. In my driveway, a place that bordered the ominous woods, there was a small curvature that acted as a slope. To learn biking(*The easiest way without injuring yourself*, my dad had said), you would simply keep the bike in motion and travel down the slope, then stop the bike by setting your feet down at the end. This included no use of the pedal. I had struggled for two days to get the hang of it. The first obstacle while learning biking(as well as most other things) is fear. It is a natural human tendency to fret over new activities. When I had begrudgingly agreed to learn biking, I started going down the hill with seven stops with my feet. I got frustrated over the slow progress and started to hate biking. I began to doubt myself over what I was doing, but when I accomplished my goal, I was satisfied, and I rejoiced. After doing twenty-five up-and-downs for two days straight, the number of stops slowly reduced, and I was able to go down the slope with zero stops. But my learning wasn't over yet. I still needed to add the pedaling part to the process. I now needed to complete the biking course by traveling across a flat surface, and I decided to do this by pedaling along the diameter of the cul-de-sac. I had gotten the hang of it on the first day of trying it myself because the driveway slope had taught me how to balance myself on the bike. *When pedaling, don't stop until you want to. Press the brakes and put your feet down to stop.* My dad had explained it to me. He had ridden a bike in India, but when he had accidentally descended down an entrance to a temple and crashed, the priests weren't happy, and therefore, he had to stop biking(his mother scolded him a lot after apologizing to the priests). On the second day of attempting to pedal, I was able to not only travel across the cul-de-sac but also exit the area and bike in the neighborhood. I enjoyed the feeling, the *click-click-click* from the continuous motion of the wheels and a slow *whirr…* when stopping. I was fond of the feel of the wind on my face as I maintained balance on two wheels, going much faster than my feet would ever carry me. Since then, I have always taken a five-minute biking break when doing homework, chores, or any other tiring activities to clear my mind. And now, my main source of transportation to meet Ernest and my other friends is the bike. My two-wheeler talent was efficient in many ways, I had discovered. Environmentally, entertainingly, and transportation-wise.

This example shows my learning process better than any other. Let me predict a likely layout for the future of this project: If I continued training, I would feel useless and experience uncertainty over my progress. Then, after a couple of days(maybe even months, depending on the activity and how much time I had to accomplish the goal), I would get used to the strain and be able to see the messages clearly. Maybe after getting used to this, I wouldn't even have to strain to intercept the messages at a farther radius. Or maybe my process of learning or my determination wouldn't work for this, and I would get the knack of this much quicker or much slower than usual. For this, only time will tell.

Chapter 20

The Long Winter

"A holiday isn't a holiday, without plenty of freedom and fun."

– Louisa May Alcott

ONE WEEK LATER
DECEMBER 17, 2018

Well, wouldn't you know it, it was already Winter break. During the holidays, I had a whole list of what I liked to do. First things first, I enjoyed the holidays' time for getting to have extra time to sleep. Otherwise, during school days, I would forcefully be awakened by an alarm clock screaming in my ear. Number two, the winter time was always cold, so we would buy a container of hot cocoa powder to make and slurp as a tasty form of warming up. Third, since we followed Jewish tradition, we would celebrate Hanukkah. My mom would make tasty latkes as a snack for this festivity, and we would spin the dreidel for some time, earning us gelt or chocolate coins. Number four, we would either go someplace for the holidays or we would go to some local places for holiday fun. This included playdates, local rides, arcade centers, classy restaurants, etc. This was probably the thing I enjoyed most on my list. And last but not least, Noah, Noemi, and I would get a gift from my parents, whether it be an amazing book series, a science activity kit, or interesting games and other puzzles that challenged and sharpened the mind. This was the case for these two weeks. Our school allotted us a two-week winter break to celebrate the holidays. For this winter break, we were going to my aunt's place in Portland. Anita Aunty *ji*, or Aunty *ji* as we would simply call her, was a beautiful woman with smooth flowing hair the color of coal, a captivating greenish-brown eye color, and a grace that could be sensed whenever she spoke in a soft, gentle voice. She grew up with my dad, and he often told me about the mischief and fun they had done together back in the day. She was an expert at *kathak*, a dance done in the northern region of India. She would occasionally show us the dance, impressing us with her elegant postures, hand and foot movements, and expressions. Her passion was followed by her husband, Karthik, who was the music part of her dance, symbolizing an excellent couple. They had two kids, Mohan and Mohini, one ten and the other seven. When calling her kids, Aunty *ji* would shout, “MoMo, come!” indicating a cute nickname for her children. They would then grumble and stomp in protest to her summoning and give a rude, “*What?*” I didn’t support the arrogant behavior toward parents, and my philosophy is that children should respect their parents. We first took an Uber to get to the airport. We waited for what felt like an hour to get checked in and officialized for the trip in line. Once that was over, we had an hour to enjoy the many coffee and snack shops the airport contained. After filling ourselves with a few bagels and some coffee, we headed over to the transit lounge to wait to board the plane. After ten minutes, a voice came on the PA: "*Flight 278 to Portland, please board the aircraft.*" Everybody in the waiting room stood up with relief as they descended into the walkway that led us to the plane. When the carpeted floor met a metal base, we knew we were about to step into the plane. We found our seats after awaiting the slow line. My mom sat with me in seats 14A and 14B, while my dad and Noemi sat in seats 15A and 15B behind us. My dad and I read books as we were midway to Portland. I always found aircraft travel quite tedious, and patience was an important quality if you had to board an airplane to travel someplace. After two hours, we reached the Portland airport, and it took us a while to leave the plane and get to the baggage claim. Once we picked up our bags, we called another Uber to drop us off at Aunty *ji*'s house. We finally reached our destination after a long wait at the airport, plane, and Uber. It was a bright house with a cottage-in-the-woods kind of vibe. We knocked on the stained glass door, and Uncle *ji* opened up. “Hi!” the overlapping voices said in unison. “Hello, Karthik!” my dad said, and Uncle *ji* patted him roughly on the back. “Where’s Anita?” he asked Uncle *ji* in Hindi. “Oh, she’s making dinner for us,” he replied. He greeted my mom, Noemi, and me and guided us to meet Mohan and Mohini, who were not so thrilled but happy to see us. We headed into the kitchen to see Aunty *ji*, and my mom and dad hugged her. We sat and conversed with them about how our lives were going, and we learned about how theirs was going, too. Noemi and I soon left the adults to their chatter and asked if we could go upstairs to see our younger cousins. When Aunty and Uncle *ji* gladly agreed, we pitter-pattered up to see Mohan moving his thumbs rapidly on a video game remote and Mohini playing with a porcelain tea set. Both were so engrossed in their entertainment that they didn’t even notice us.

"Uh, hi, guys…" Noemi interrupted the moment awkwardly. Both took a glance at us and continued their play. "Nathan *bhaiyya*, come and play this game with me! It's so fun!" he said, eyes glued to the screen. *Bhaiyya* was an informal way to say "brother" in Hindi. I silently trudged over to the couch where Mohan was seated, and Noemi walked over to sit where Mohini was playing with her tea set. I took control of the extra remote control that was attached to the TV. It was a car racing game, typical for a ten-year-old to play it. Once we selected the two-player option, Mohan eagerly showed me how to control the car. I nodded, but I wasn't really getting a good grasp on it. When the race started, Mohan zoomed off, and I stood trying to maneuver it. "Move the joystick forward, Nathan!" he said without looking. I did as he said, and off I went. I bolted across the artificial cityscape, and I frequently ran into light posts and or buildings, then reversed and continued the race. Mohan bit his tongue as he raced beside me and bumped his car into mine. “Gotcha!” he yelled with triumph. My downtrodden car took a moment to start; then, I proceeded at a speed of 50 MPH. Of course, Mohan won, and considered it a big pride to win against an older opponent. “You know, I don’t play video games all the time.” I said in defense. He shrugged and browsed for another game to play. “Actually, Mohan, you should do something else with me other than gaming.” He didn’t seem thrilled by the idea and dragged his feet across the white carpet while I searched for a board game to play. I found an abandoned Jumanji lurking in the corner of a closet and pulled it out. I set up the game and then asked Noemi and Mohini if they wanted to join. I knew Noemi didn’t really want to play Jumanji, but she was relieved to be free from the boring pretend tea game she was playing. Since Mohini’s pretend-play partner deserted her, she hopped over to join us. I explained the rules, and we began. To me, entertainment was very important, especially when it came to board games. During vacation, my family would bring along one of our favorite board games or buy a game from the place we were vacationing in. For example, when we visited Hawaii when I was in the second grade, we bought these Hawaiian-styled playing cards called “Kūkulu” cards. They were regular playing cards with Hawaiian words on them, although it didn’t say the meaning of the words. That vacation was very important to me; I don’t think I’ve ever had a vacation where I’ve felt so *calm* and *tranquil* before. For all I knew, if my power *ever* went away, I could meditate in solitude in the Kauai Hindu Monastery.

We usually liked to play chess(only my dad and I knew how to play), Monopoly, Ludo, Snakes n’ Ladders, and card games like Memory, Go Fish, Crazy 8’s, etc. My family and I found the most entertaining time when we played Monopoly, so my dad, Noemi, and I pieced together a hexagonal Monopoly board and called it “World Monopoly.” Each of the six sides represented the six inhabited continents. Instead of buying extra materials for constructing the other parts of the Monopoly, for example, the property/rent cards, the tokens, and the pawns, we printed out the house/hotel cards and the Wild Property cards, which acted as the WTO and UN cards. We bought better acrylic coins for tokens and used Ludo pieces as pawns. For properties, we used color-coded pushpins and put them on the properties we own, and we would put a small Lego tower for purchasing hotels and wider Lego blocks for ports.

As we were halfway through the game, and when we all had lost at least one life token, Aunty *ji* called us down for dinner. Mohan grumbled, “Five minutes, Mom!” I said, “Actually, Noemi and I were planning to head downstairs. I think your mom would like it if you came with us.” I offered. The siblings looked at each other and shrugged. We all came downstairs, and Aunty *ji* was surprised to see her children so soon after she had called for them. “What happened to ‘five minutes,’ Mohan?” she asked with a smile. Mohan rolled his eyes. We were served scrumptious Mediterranean cuisine, and I devoured the falafels and baba ganoush. After a filling meal, we continued the game of Jumanji we left off. Mohini won the game soon after, leaving her puzzled as to how she could win a game she was not interested in. “That was a nice game,” she murmured shyly with a lisp. Aunty *ji* showed us to a guest bedroom with two bunk beds for four people to rest on. We were delighted by the hospitality, and we all snoozed after the food made us drowsy. My dad took the top bunk, I took the bottom one, and so did Mom and Noemi on the other side. As I tried to get some sleep, I thought about the suspicious messages I had received in the hotel room that night and how life after that seemed weirder and weirder. Well, hopefully, this mystery will be untangled soon.

I woke up early because Uncle *ji* wanted to show us some attractions in Portland. So, we all got ready and flocked to museums, botanical gardens, zoos, bookstores, and many other places that amazed the eye. We ate lunch at the Oregon Zoo, and it was evening before we returned. Aunty *ji* made us some tasty Thai, and I munched with delight on the spongy tofu in the red curry and slurped my greasy noodles. With a full stomach yet our entertainment capacity only half-full, we all played a game of dumb charades. Someone would go up and stop speaking and instead signal to everyone to guess what movie they were referring to. There were different signals that would tell you which language, time period, and how many words there were in the title. Then, they would try to give clues about the name of the movie, with either action scenes from the movie(without any sound, of course) or act out what the movie title's words were. For example, for *King Kong*, someone might stomp around beating their chest or behave like a king, then like an ape. These would hint at the movie's name, and the first person to call out the name would go next. Like this, dumb charades was a game that could continue for as long as you wanted.

We slept at around eleven after all the fun. The next few days continued this way, enjoying our time in Portland with Aunty *ji* and her family. But then, after the vacation had made me forget about my daily life's troubles, I suddenly traced some other suspicious messages. My power was always interrupting my entertainment time. Even last Thanksgiving break, those texts made me ponder on them so much that my fun was gone. Why were the odd messages intervening when I traveled? Is it our fault that my family keeps going to dubious places? Or do the dubious places go wherever *I go*?

Unknown User:

12-11-8 44-8-1 22-4-5 65-3-7 59-10-8

Boss:

34-8-6 45-3-2 86-9-7 69-15-4 39-12-6 76-8-4 97-14-1 110-7-8 53-9-3 4-1-5 18-5-9

I had seen this kind of numeric code in Vulture and the principal's messages. What could it mean? How could I decode it? Right before the break, Ernest had agreed to assist me in advancing my capabilities, but he also agreed to find out about the suspicious messages being sent to one another and how that's related to all the changes happening around us. These peculiar messages were one of the reasons why I sought Ernest's aid. But since it was all unrelated digits to me, I decided to ignore it. It would save me the little remains I had of mental peace.

After a week and a half of spending some time with my aunt, uncle, and cousins, we bade our farewell and flew back to good old Livermore. I found out that I am unable to intercept messages through gaming servers, which made me feel insecure and, at the same time, relieved. Since I usually get a holiday gift from my parents and didn't think that *Santa* would come and give it to me, I decided to request a present this time. I asked my parents for an Xbox for my holiday gift, which perplexed them as to why I would ask for a video game. Since they knew I wasn't the gaming type, they really got concerned and started to talk to me about finishing all of my assignments and chores and then getting on the gaming console, but I assured them it was only for entertainment when my friends came over. When I got the game, I still couldn't sense the messages, no matter how much concentration I applied. It was as if I was the big bad wolf, and it made no difference how much I "huffed and puffed" to see the message; the house wouldn't blow away. I tried touching multiple parts of the game, including the gamepad, the screen, and the wires, but the same emptiness appeared. Suddenly, a sharp burning sensation hit my hand, and I recoiled. I opened my eyes to see wires smoking and sizzling and occasional crackles and zaps of electricity. Oops. I had applied too much power, and the game got fried. This could be useful if properly controlled. What would I tell my parents? What would be my story? When should I tell them? After a lot of mental questioning, I finally came up with an answer. I would reveal it during dinner(that is if my parents were in a good mood), and I would back it up with "Just fiddling with the wires."

My mom was excited as she selected a gift for Vidya's 12th birthday party, twirling around the room as she put the gift in a pink bag with unicorns all over it. Vidya was one of our family friends, and we would always attend her birthday parties during the winter break. She put a note in it that said, "*From Nathan, Noemi, Sofia, and Anil.*" Her ear-to-ear smile was so infectious that even I smiled, although I felt *something* was off. I had not been intercepting any messages about the party during the day. Typically, Seema Auntie would text my mom and ask her to stay after the party or tell her that she would see her there. No activity whatsoever. I hesitated to come along, but soon enough, I was in the car, going to Penny's Playhouse. Penny's Playhouse was a place illuminated with pink party lights and games everywhere you went(except for the bathrooms, *which* would be a little suspicious). There was a large, inflated playhouse with an obstacle course for children of all ages. There was a rock-climbing wall opposite the Playhouse and a bumper car and laser tag center adjacent to that. 4D experience rides, dart games, and other aiming games stood in the center of the buffoonery palace. Right in front of these games were the arcade games, where video game addicts and skillful screen people hung out. A high ropes course was above the games, and daring children and adults strapped themselves up and made careful steps across the course. All in all, this place was the dream for kids who wanted to take a break from their working lives(which weren't *really* working lives), exert their physical energy, and show excitement. I had a different idea of a break, but many people would find my definition too boring.

When we reached, the front desk lady, a short young blonde, had asked us to fill out a digital waiver to get signed up. My mom didn't appreciate the inconvenience, yet she still spent the time doing so. When we reached there, we saw a large group of Desi people, which was normal for a party arranged by an Indian family. We searched the entire area for Vidya, Roshan, Rahul Uncle, or Seema Auntie, but they were not to be seen. My mom was puzzled, but I could see what was happening. My mom asked the front desk lady if this was Vidya's birthday party, and they said yes, which confused me. Tired and mystified, we sat down on a nearby bench. A quick-paced footstep came our way. We saw the front-desk lady approach us, and she stated, "Actually, I don't see a 'Vidya' registered here." My mom showed the lady the invitation. The lady commented, pointing to the invitation. "It says Friday, December 28." My mom slapped her head but was smiling, clearly amused with herself. The lady said, "You're welcome to stay if you want!" in an attempt to encourage us, obviously trying to increase their business by saying so. It didn't seem like anybody visited Penny's Playhouse nowadays. "No, I think we're okay." my mom reassured her. Noemi had already stood in the queue for the laser tag, but my mom urged her to come with us. "We're leaving *already*?" Noemi responded, but my mom said she would tell her in the car. As we sat down in the car, my mom sighed. There was a moment of silence, then both of us started to laugh our heads off. My mom chortled so loudly that even Noemi joined in without even knowing what the situation was. We called my dad, who was at work. "*Hello Sofia, how did the party go?*" my dad asked innocently.

We began cackling even louder.

"*Um, can someone tell me what exactly happened?*"

We told the story about the birthday party and how it was not even Vidya's birthday that day. My dad started to laugh, too. He said, "*Well, at her real birthday party, you can tell Seema and Rahul that you were so excited to come; you came a week beforehand.*"

My mom agreed and then asked my dad if we could go to Schlotzsky's for dinner.

After a nice week and a half in Portland, along with an accidental Xbox screw-up, goofing up birthday parties, and unusual codes, I thought my winter break was pretty sweet. We finished the simple vacation with grandeur. We stayed up until 12:00 to celebrate the new year with leftover fireworks and sparklers from Diwali. 2019, another year of messages and misery.

Chapter 21

Pointless Birthday "Festivities"

"A birth-date is a reminder to celebrate the life as well as to update the life."

– Amit Kalantri

A FEW MONTHS LATER
FEBRUARY 15, 2019

A lot has happened since the time I first started to train with Ernest. A few days after we practiced first on the soccer field, Ernest showed me some functions on his phone that seemed to be disabled, like the buttons weren't working the way they should. We connected the dots, and we realized that if I strained my ability, the functioning of the device system would be jinxed up. It was pretty cool. I just had to make a mental note, "*Uh, come on, brain, struggle,*" and a phone would break, or a game would incinerate. It wasn't gravity's fault that Mom's phone fell. It was *my* power(no offense, Newton). It's not like that was a good thing, anyway. My power, *my* fault. And Noemi has slowly started to back away from "The Phone Mystery." One headache gone, a million more to go. Well, besides the accidental mess-up of devices, ever since Ernest discovered I was capable of this, he has made me train on it. He figured it would be a good offensive tactic if we ever got into trouble. I can also sense messages within a half-mile radius. I should give myself a pat on the back. Not bad. I could also filter out the top priority messages from the unnecessary messages. In this way, my mind is balanced, and I don't crowd it. I only had to completely engross myself in the activity I was doing so the unimportant messages would be ignored, and the messages with keywords and codes would not be ignored. All thanks to Ernest for being so cooperative. That was what you call a true friend. Ernest had also found out about a place in which our work could be safely executed. Since most of the perpetrators were amongst school staff, Ernest had explored the outside of the school and found the janitors' supply room. This was a safe place to visit after 5:00 when they were done cleaning. I had to get used to the smell of strong bleach. Over there, I would try to intercept any messages coming from teachers. I assumed many had to do work after school, so it was a good time. Since we took our school devices to set up our message-intercepting and translating database(it was convenient to do it that way, in case we ever forgot to bring our devices back), Ernest had developed a way to prevent any computer activity from being seen by our teachers. Now, we couldn't be tracked, and we could do our work in stopping crime without any reveal. Sure makes me glad to have a hacker as a friend.

In all this time, I've also thought, being a "philosopher,"

what is *power*? What does power necessarily imply to someone? Why does a normal kid with a normal life need this power? Power is like a Yin-Yang. It has pros and cons, and it can be used for good and evil alike. It really got me thinking. As I thought about mature and more plausible things related to my skill, the more I thought about the *immature*, stupid things. For example, I have seen many movies where people get "charged" by lightning or electricity and become more powerful. Could that work for me? I know it was a fictitious, unrealistic power source, but even my power seemed fictitious and unrealistic, right? Could I enhance my power by taking my vitamins daily, like my mom asked me to do? At least I could save myself from her scolding. What about extra physical activity or spending more time outside? Or practicing my violin more in an attempt to train my third hemisphere with calming music?

I didn't look at myself like a superhero just because I had this quirk. Sure, I certainly help people, but superheroes can be anyone who helps society in bad times, like doctors or police. I told myself I was too old to like superheroes anymore, yet I still had posters of them on my bedroom walls. Although I certainly liked superheroes, I had many different thoughts and analyses on them. The "superpower" superheroes glorify themselves, and I don't want to do that. Anyway, here is a list of my favorite superheroes and why I like them.

1. Iron Man: Iron Man is the perfect example of a normal guy who makes a lot of money yet still gets to have fun as a superhero. He has an interesting story and an important role in the Avengers, yet he is a fun and easy-going character.
2. Thor: I love to read about many different types of cultures and what they believe in, and since Thor is a character from Norse mythology, I like him a lot. Plus, the way Chris Hemsworth portrays him in the

movies and his control of thunder and lightning.

3. Dr. Strange: Dr. Strange has a unique and amazing power; as a sorcerer, he can shift between dimensions. His sorcery can be used for defensive and offensive purposes, inter-dimensional transportation, and much more!

4. Black Panther: As I had mentioned earlier when I was explaining Thor, I love to learn about other cultures and their significance. Black Panther is very strategic, and his movies are action-packed. There is one flaw, though; in the movie, M'Baku says, "Glory to Hanuman." and Hanuman is a Hindu god.

5. Hulk: Hulk is humorous yet humongous. If you had just seen Hulk's gigantic green monster form, you would think he was a savage beast who wanted to smash everything. But, in his sane, normal, not-so-colossal-and-less-terrifying form, he is a gamma radiation scientist who provides useful info and helps the Avengers. He's the one who fights the massive

monsters while the others assist him in doing so.

Ernest and I made a huge bulletin board on all of the messages I've encountered that were related to the scheming in the hotel, and we've collected some clues. Some of the messages were traced to locations in warehouses, some of which include a hardware store in Portland, Oregon, and a factory in Berlin, Germany. They are very random places, but I feel they've got some importance. We found messages about something called the "Dexeplin Association," otherwise referred to as the "DA." I was sure Morty had passed because of some mishap with the potency or ingredients, but we needed to prove it. "Next step," Ernest addressed, "hire a private detective. Your 'friend' Ibrahim Ayyad is on the suspect board. We need to get someone to get us some of his conversations and other info." It was a good idea, but it came with risks. What if we were traced back to the private detective? I reassured myself that that was pretty unlikely, considering that Ernest had a secure system set up.

At school, the number of people using the Dexeplin pills had increased, and it itched me that this illicit business thrived. I knew I couldn't make any assumptions, but something about it did seem illegal to me, especially after Morty's passing. When I reached language arts, Ms. Lynn said, "Class, everyone wish Nathan a very happy birthday!"

I was confused at first, but then I checked the date. February 15. My birthday. My mind was so engrossed in this mystery that I had forgotten about my birthday! "HAPPY BIRTHDAY, NATHAN!!!" the class shouted in a somewhat dissonant tone. The reason that the class never *sings* "Happy Birthday" is because people ruined the song with insults in it. After that, the teachers became *extra* careful about birthday wishes. "Today, we will be doing my favorite activity!" Ms. Lynn exclaimed. "5-MINUTE ESSAYS!"

"*Ugh... come on...*" the class murmured. "Eh, don't be such downers; this skill is very important. Try your best; these are the topics." the teacher said. She started to write on the whiteboard:

Western Expansion of the United States

Cotton Candy Production in the 1970's

Maintaining a Healthy Balance of Time

Science Fiction: Steampunk

Telecommunication Advancements

Learning a New Language(Pros and Cons)

Public Speaking and Why It's Important

Poetry of Any Kind

"Since there are..." she made a mental count. "Thirty-eight kids in this class, so five people for seven of each topic, and the remaining topic will have three people writing, and that one will be..." she skimmed through her list. "Public

Speaking and Why It's Important! I will call out names and select a topic for you."

Some students mumbled, "*They're not even optional; this is so boring.*" I wondered which one of these I would get, but maybe, since it was my birthday, the teacher would show partiality towards me and give me an optional choice. Eh, don't think too highly of yourself, Nathan. "And, now, the birthday boy," Ms. Lynn announced. "Hmm, let's see. You can do telecommunication advancements." It was good because that was what I wanted. I wanted to learn anything related to my "phenomenon." While researching, I asked myself, "*If I was born in the 19th century, would I be able to sense telegraphs and other means of communication?*" Anyhow, I was born in the 21st century, so I shouldn't waste my time thinking about that and rather focus on organizing my writing. I only had five minutes.

After reaching my house, I opened my backpack to clean out my lunch container and water bottle. But *something* was odd. *None* of the things in this backpack belonged to me. There was a purple lunch box with butterfly designs on it. *My* lunchbox had a military camo color to it. My water bottle was blue and metallic, but this one was plastic and red. I raised an eyebrow and stared at the backpack, puzzled. But then I realized what had happened. I happened to have switched backpacks with Betty, one of the non-pretentious girls in my Spanish class. Uh-oh. How do I know what she must be doing with my things? I had my name written on my lunchbox, as well as my water bottle. I informed my dad about the situation, and he shrugged. "You could send an email," he suggested. I opened up my computer, put my glasses on, and started typing. Since the purpose didn't need to be formal like my other emails to the drug dealers, I didn't really have to write my words carefully or give too much thought to it.

Good Afternoon Betty,

I believe we have accidentally switched backpacks. When and where would be the best time to meet?

Regards,

Nathan

Ernest would be coming over any minute, and I wanted to discuss my third hemisphere with him and not waste any time. Surprisingly, I got a response immediately.

I was also about to email you. You can send me your address, and I will drop by sometime to switch backpacks with you.

I replied to the email with my address, and soon enough, a black SUV pulled up in the cul-de-sac. I was afraid for a second, as the government officials' car taste tended to skew towards these types of vehicles. Betty exited the front door of the van, my backpack held in her hand. I handed hers over, and we expressed our gratitude with a brief "thank you." Out of courtesy, she wished me a happy birthday once again, and she left. Should I have been polite? I was having a birthday party, but that was only with close friends and family. I hadn't informed anybody of my birthday party except for Ernest and Ethan, my two close school friends. I got rid of the awkward mind battle and entered my modest home. I then sat on the living room couch, anticipating Ernest's arrival.

Ernest and I stuck boiling-hot spring rolls into maroon soy sauce and crunched as we called the person of interest. Ernest had told me that he owed a favor to Ernest for saving his job and recovering some important files that he had lost. He was an identity tracker and private detective. *Mr. Blanc*, he had said. Ernest was planning to ask him to track Ibby for a couple of days and send audio clips and other information through email. Ernest was going to stay over for my birthday party, and his family would arrive soon. Before Ernest ate another spring roll, I said, "You might not want to eat that. I think it's going to be a pretty big cake." Although the cake was big, the amount of people coming wasn't. Just a handful of our close family and friends. Thankfully, I was not a thick-headed high school oaf who thought his parents were nobody and invited the whole school to his house for his birthday, got everybody sloshed with fruit punch, and left his house filled with garbage. The doorbell began to ring, and people started to arrive. After a nice dinner my mom made, it was time to cut the cake. After the obnoxious "Happy Birthday" song, when it was time to blow the candles, my mom whispered in my ear, "*Go on, make a wish.*" Well, what else did I want other than for my powers to go away? I mean, actually, I've found out that my powers are useful and that they can help so many people. That's it! "I wish the world was rid of problems and innocent people stopped suffering because of global issues. I *wish* the world was at peace." Everyone clapped, and twelve candles with dainty little flames flickered and disappeared in a blow.

The number of people using the drug felt like it had quadrupled since the time I came back from Thanksgiving Break. Before every class, people popped a pill in their mouths. The teachers also began to notice F's turn to C minuses and C minuses turn to A pluses and were perplexed as to how this was happening. It was funny; they barbated us on "how you should pay attention" and "focus real hard," and they themselves didn't pay attention to how their pupils' grades suddenly skyrocketed. Unfortunately, the company making the drug didn't seem to understand that if kids get addicted to the drugs, it could affect the kids in a bad way, as well as their business. When they took their medication, they would focus for that time of the day, and then either have sporadic bursts of energy or just be drowsy the rest of the day. I hoped no one else would end up like Morty. In history class, Ernest sat beside me as we took notes from the lecture on the Cold War. I whispered, "*Hey, Ernest, why do we really need to learn history? I mean, don't people say focus on the present, not the past?*" He didn't respond at first, trying to finish up his notes, then said, "*That's a common FAQ. Haven't you heard the saying, 'Those who fail to learn history are doomed to repeat it.'?*"

I said, "*Teachers probably made that up to keep students away from boredom.*" with a smirk.

Ernest added, "*Actually, Winston Churchill said that.*"

"*Oh.*"

After a short pop quiz, we parted ways for our separate classes. As I just entered Mrs. Gowda's classroom, Danny and his oversized goons blocked me, their bodies towering over me like the Great Wall of China. Danny yelled, "Hey, Dawson, come here! You and Bauer are going to have a *lot* of explaining to do. Got it?!" He held us by the shirt and dragged us to the maintenance room.

The only thing I *could* see through this armpit-smelling bag on my head was the dim light of the maintenance. I felt my hands being tied to a pole, and I grunted. The bag was removed, and I saw Ernest adjacent to me, tied up in the same way. Danny stood in front of me, toothpick in his mouth, a wicked scowl on his face. He spit his toothpick on the ground next to me, and I gulped. He began to speak. "So, boys, all you gotta do is tell me *why* you did it. Then you're outta this mess, and we can forget about all this baloney." Ernest and I shared a glance, scared. If we told him how we got him suspended, what if that provoked him and got him to

torture us? I said, "Untie us, and we'll speak." He considered this for a moment, then punched me in the face. I cringed, tasting blood in my mouth. I croaked, "*I won't repeat what I said.*" Danny sighed, then shrugged. He signaled for his buddies to untie us. I smiled. This was going to be fun. Now untied, I concentrated on his cell phone, and it cracked in his pocket. He looked to see what happened, and that was my moment. I swiftly delivered a kick to the (you know where). His eyes bulged, he gagged, and just stood there, frozen. I fell to the floor and pretended to have fainted. Survival Skills 101. Ernest did the same, and afterward, loudly shrieked, "HELP!! HELP!! We're here! Help!!!" and also pretended to pass out. People heard, and soon, a teacher came in and took us out of the room; the whole sixth grade gathered around to see the commotion. This was going to be really bad for Danny's student profile. At least we won't expect any more business with that dude. I was pretty sure I could have caused the phone to catch flames if I concentrated enough. But I'll save that for the *real deal*.

As I looked for Ernest later that day, I saw him walk up to me in brown rags, bent down like a cripple, with a long white beard and walking stick. I had hoped that whatever Danny did to him didn't cause him any mental injury. He said in an old, hoarse voice,

"*Beware the Jabberwock, my son! The jaws that bite, the claws that catch! Beware the Jubjub bird, and shun the frumious Bandersnatch!*"

He made 'claws' with his fingers and a very idiotic monster face. I stammered, not knowing how to react. "Um… nice, so…"

He said with a smile, "Pretty convincing, right? We're doing a play in drama on the nonsensical poem 'Jabberwocky' by Lewis Carroll, as well as two other plays." I gave a thumbs-up, then said, "We really are the talk of the school now. I know we were so thrilled when we designed

SpectersCloak23, but that's mysterious attention. This is what *actual* attention is. I don't really like it as much." Ernest gave a "me too" kind of nod, kind of headshake. He spoke abruptly, "By the way, I'm supposed to give you this." He handed me an invitation to the school play next week. The play was supposed to be hosted in our neighboring and competing school, Reagan Middle School, named after the former president. I folded it and kept it in my shirt pocket. "Hey, um, Nathan?" I heard Danny's voice behind us. We turned and saw Danny limping around from the injury. "I know I've been a big jerk, and I'm just here to say I'm sorry. When you somehow revealed my cheating, I know you were doin' the right thing. Anybody would have done the same. I shouldn't have ganged up on ya." He scratched his head. "From now on, if you need anything, my buddies and I are here to help. I owe that to you."

We also apologized for hurting him, and he left after the awkward forgiveness moment. Ernest's phone buzzed, and as he went to reach it, he stopped. “Oh yeah, I don’t need to look at it. I have you.” “*Using his resources, huh?*” I thought.

Mr. Blanc:

I have sent you all the information I could gather in these couple of days. Attached are the files below:

“Mr. Blanc sent you what he learned from spying on Ibby,” I informed Ernest. “We’ll have to check it out later,” Ernest said and waved as we parted ways to head to our next period.

After school, we headed to Ernest’s shed outside his house. We parked our bikes and headed towards the half-broken, unmaintained place. It was a place used for the storage of unwanted things, such as kids’ toys, old electronics and furniture, and many other things worth putting in an antique collection. After digging through the area, we found many vintage valuables that might give us some profit if we sold them. The half-peeled wallpaper and broken tiles gave it a creepy vibe. Ernest turned on the system of monitors he had set up and went to check SpectersCloak23's inbox. We opened up one of the audio clips that he had sent us, and we got what we were looking for:

"Agent Blanc, 7:00 P.M. Sunday, February 17, 2019, Espionage target's residence." We knew we had hired the best because nobody else really bothered to give this kind of information.

"Hello, Lloyd. Thank you for coming here on such short notice." We heard the deep voice and Arab accent of Mr. Ayyad.

"No problem, Ibby. I have the requested files and the copies you asked me to bring. Whom should I submit this to?" That was the voice of our principal, Mr. Davenport, which only proved that teachers were getting their hands dirty.

“You can hand it over to me for now, and then I’ll give it to my boss, Kelly Robinson. Isn’t it funny? She turned out to be your boss in the DA and in your job. I pity you.” Well, I don’t know if our principal liked his barb, but what could he do? His boss was Ibby, and he couldn’t give back.

“Also, Lloyd, we have been given some dough to prevent any pharma companies from testing the pill. Make sure our scientists are submitting the usual report.”

The clip ended shortly after they said their farewells. The same questions spun through our minds. *Why did the files need copies? Were they for emergencies, or did they have a purpose? Why didn’t they want their pill to be tested? Why were all these teachers and other academic officials entering this corrupt field?*

“We need to use SpectersCloak23 one more time. And this will be payback for all the stupid rules we have to follow at school because we’re gonna bust the freaking superintendent of our school district." I declared, determined.

Chapter 22

The Non-"Bay Area" Area

"Blackmail is more effective than bribery."

– John le Carré

In school, we had a field trip to The Banks & Baker Farm in Pueblo Sureño, a small area between Livermore and Pleasanton. Strangely enough, although Livermore and Pleasanton shared very liberal views, this specific area was a high-crime, poor, conservative-viewed area. It was not really a "Bay Area" kind of place. The school, sharing the majority of the political views of Livermore, ensured the safety of all the sixth graders and asked permission from the students' parents. My dad had given me an iron rod to put in my field trip bag. "Use it when you have no other choice, whether it may be used to jab the guy in the gut, bludgeon his head, or gouge out his eyes. And don't worry about getting thrown into jail for homicide; we'll win the case in court. We'll say it was an act of *self-defense*." he said dramatically, and then I convinced him that my school would give everyone absolute security, with the local police accompanying us. I generally liked field trips for the long bus rides, where I could see more of Livermore and Pleasanton suburbs and poorer areas. Since the field trip was for the zoology unit in science, science classes were paired together and were grouped into different buses, with each bus having two to three classes. Thankfully, my bus had Ernest and Ethan's class, so we sat next to each other and chatted the whole way there. When we reached, I could understand why my teachers were cautious about the students. Everyone walking nearby was *staring* at us, staring with utter disapproval. There was a man, fat with a brown beard, with a hat and boots, carrying a large rifle. The local police started to gather around the students. "Howdy, little peeps. Ain't gonna blast ya', don't worry. Just gonna hunt in the woods for a lil' while." the man said.

"Joe, there's a government permit on the woods now. You can't go hunting there, or the Wildlife Department could get you to serve more time. You don't want more on your record." a policeman said.

Joe shrugged. "Well, I ain't goin' back home without a nice game for supper."

His challenging attitude terrified the students, and that was the last we saw of him as he sat in handcuffs in a police jeep. "Well, kids, not to worry, that's all taken care of." a lady said. She was wearing a tucked-in checkered shirt, breeches, shiny Texan boots, and a belt with a star in the center. A total cowgirl. "Hi, my name is Sandra, and I will be your tour guide for The Banks & Baker Farm." She showed us to a gallery of historical portraits and paintings and explained to us how a group of people from Texas immigrated to California during the Gold Rush, trying to find new settlements there for better business and lifestyle. There, Charles Smith "Smitty" Baker and William Jameson Banks founded The Banks & Baker Farm and started to raise livestock and crops, then sell them for profit. Other people started owning the company and its shares over time, and now it is owned by a man named Emmanuel Martinez and the descendant of Mr. Banks, Julia Banks. Then Sandra paired each science class with another tour guide to take them to other sites on the farm. Our tour guide was a cheerful, hyperactive woman named MJ. "This is our longhorn farm, and as you can see, they certainly sport *really big* horns, with most having four feet or less and some up to six to eight feet. The average weight of the horns is fifteen to twenty pounds. Our longhorns have tags on their ears which—"

Suddenly, a gunshot was heard. A commotion was going on outside of the barn. "*Q-Quickly get inside.*" MJ quivered. We ran inside the barn and grouped up with all the other science classes, the teachers doing accurate yet intense attendance recording. Since it was almost about to be lunchtime, the teachers allowed us to open up our lunches while we hid from the danger. My mom had packed me taquitos and some chips in the paper bag where my lunch was stored. As I was eating, I heard Mr. Nuñez ask our TA(teacher's assistant), Baxter, to get his sandwich. When Baxter returned, he got a bottle of soap, likely from the bathroom. Mr. Nuñez was confused. "Um… Baxter, *why* exactly do you have soap instead of my lunch?" Baxter was befuddled. "But Mr. Nuñez, you told me to get hand wash, right?"

Mr. Nuñez shook his head. "No, Baxter, I asked you to get my *sandwich*, not *hand wash*." Baxter had recently been experiencing ear problems and deafness, which was apparent by the way he was slapping at his ears as he went to retrieve the teacher's lunch. I assumed somebody else would be the TA now.

The field trip soon resumed, and MJ made us fill out a chart of the classification of animals(specifically longhorns) and made us write some notes on the adaptations and characteristics of the longhorns and the other livestock that were there. Then we switched stations with other groups, picking up more information about crop growth, classification, and adaptations, and we learned about how they fermented their own beer and wine, which is now a local brand called “Vaqueros y Granjeros: Irish Red Ale.” We never even got to try even a small sip, even though most beers have less alcohol than a spoon of cough syrup. It’s a good thing that the commotion happened because the field trip hosts had to wrap up quickly, and I never got to see this dreaded crime-filled non-*Bay Area* area again.

Today, I was heading over to Reagan Middle School after school with my parents to see the school play that Ernest was participating in. Since we were nearing the end of the school year, the teachers jam-packed the end of the year with "fun" activities, which included the field trip and this play. But this play was *far* from fun. Instead of being invited with confetti, *we* were invited with water balloons that wet our clothes. "Sofia, calm down! It was just a little prank!" My father tried to calm my mother's rage. "THEY CAN'T JUST PUT WATER ON US AND EXPECT US TO BE QUIET!!! I SHOULD'VE GIVEN THEM A NICE SPANKING AS SOON I SAW THEM!!!"

There was another commotion going on, a couple of jerks from Reagan Middle School who hated Livermore Middle.

"Well, lions can be bitten by rattlesnakes." one of the boys, Luke, said. He had that smart-aleck kind of smirk, which everybody hated except for his goons.

"Lions and rattlesnakes don't even live in the same place, you dumb Reagan Rabbits!"

"Who cares, Livermore Lizards!"

They were quarreling idiotically and quite pointlessly over the school mascots. The dialogue soon started to become physical, from shoving all the way to a fistfight. Luke sneaked away from the fighting so he couldn't get in trouble. Crack-brained imbecile. The teachers came in to stop the fighting. After everybody was seated, the play began. It started with a play based on the Jabberwocky, with Ernest playing a small role as an old man. Mrs. Dawson was in tears to see her beloved son on stage. Ernest announced, "And hast thou slain the Jabberwock? Come to my arms, my beamish boy!"

Suddenly, something flew from the audience and in Ernest's face. Pieces of an eggshell fell to the ground. More snickers from the boys. First of all, how and *why* would that guy bring an egg to school just to joke around? Not funny at all. Those kids were *surely* going to be suspended. Ernest gave them a dirty scowl, wiped his face on his ridiculous costume, and continued. After the play ended, another play started, and it was after the famous book by Rudyard Kipling, "The Jungle

Book." People dressed in colorful clothes depicting animals danced around the stage. Ernest was Baloo, the bear, but he was way too frail and bony to be a large, bulky creature. As the play continued and came to its climax, another set of disasters occurred. Suddenly, ground spinners, which were basically fireworks that were on the ground, started bursting and filled the auditorium with erupting sound. Balloons burst behind the stage actors, and their costumes were filled with paint that was inside the balloons. Of course, after that, the play was canceled. The staff were trying to find out who lit the fireworks, although I thought it was pretty obvious.

After the series of ever-so-dramatic events, including the actual stage drama, I couldn't meet Ernest, so we joined a Zoom meeting, and I screen-shared my email to the superintendent:

February 19, 2019

SpectersCloak23
Specterscloak23@gmail.com
ADDRESS CLASSIFIED

Kelly Robinson
kelly.robinson@lvusd.net
5309 Purple Pond Court

Good Evening,

You must know who I am because of my history in Livermore Middle School, but still, I shall introduce myself. I am SpectersCloak23, the online policeman. I know about your fraudulent business in the pharmaceutical industry, and I would like some information about the founder of the Dexeplin Association. If you do not give me the needed information, I will inform the local police as well as the FBI, and you will serve a long and hard sentence. So, please do what is needed.

Regards,
SpectersCloak23

Before sending it, I asked Ernest if I needed to add anything. He said, "You have nothing to add. It's exactly what we want in the exact words." I sent the email, and we logged out of the meeting. I found the whole "online policeman" thing very humorous. I used the short amount of time afterward to practice violin. I had a concert in the spring and was practicing "Remember Me," a song from the Disney movie "Coco" for performance. When I came down for supper, the main discussion was March Madness. Although this day and age is more into football than anything, I still am big into basketball. When my parents came to America for college, they came to North Carolina, the hubbub of basketball. My mom and dad had first met there, at the University of North Carolina at Chapel Hill. They went to college basketball games, and the whole family has been a huge fan(except Noemi, who never liked us going there for basketball). Noah and I still have dunk duels and hoop head-to-heads. I am always more of a bookworm, but I do like other sports and find them interesting. My top four after basketball are tennis, cricket, soccer, and swimming, respectively. Even though

I would only start tennis lessons in the summer, I had already begun to watch videos of previous games and how to play. Cricket, a sport introduced to me by my dad, was my third favorite sport, which I would play with him outside before dinner(or basketball). It required immense concentration, as my dad was an expert bowler. I didn't know how to play soccer, but I found the game entertaining to watch, and it was something to discuss with my friends every time the World Cup came along. Swimming is a sport I mainly enjoy during the summer, as it is a form of exercise, but it is very refreshing during the summer heat. All of my family members enjoyed using the pool in the summertime, especially my mom. She *loved* swimming. I didn't like doing sports during PE, mainly because of Coach Vencer. He always encouraged the heftier kids to bully the weaker kids and said in defense, "Well, bud, it's not my problem that *you're* frail and disabled." Says the person who doesn't move an inch during the class period. To him, everybody would be frail!

The next day, Ernest asked me, “Did you get a reply from Mrs. Robinson?” I shrugged. “I’ll check that first thing after school,” I stated. The school was presenting the awards to the drama teachers and students for their stage performance yesterday. The school apologized on behalf of Reagan Middle School for disrupting the play, so all the theater students got to get special privileges for today. This *isn’t* right. The kids who did that yesterday *should* be apologizing rather than our teachers doing this. After school, I got off the bus, the growling motor emitting an acrid gasoline smell. The bus zoomed away from Sherwood Court, and I knocked on the door. My mom answered it. “Nathan, do you want to go with me for a quick stop to Walmart?” Usually, when my mom said “quick” stop to Walmart, she meant really long, tedious, and boring. Luckily, I could interpret that. But since I was done with all my homework, I didn't have much to do. So, I agreed to her offer. There, the most unexpected thing happened. Luke, the jerk who was pulling all those pranks off, was in the dairy section, fingers to his head, his eyes closed tightly. What was he doing? Why was he here, doing this nonsense? The lights started to flicker, and then stopped. He was chewing something, probably his trademark lime-flavored gum, and smirked slyly like he knew *everything* and *anything* that would happen.

After buying what we needed, my mom took me to Great Clips to get a haircut. I always found haircuts to be very annoying and uncomfortable while your hair was being cut, but the result was amazing and impeccable. Thankfully, our favorite barber Wang was there. He always did my hair just like I wanted it. Although, he didn't do his *own* hair as neat as his clients. The back side of his hair was very spiky, the front side neat, and he had a bald spot in the middle of the chaos. Wang was busy cutting someone's hair, his hands moving swiftly, comb and scissors working like magic. He stopped suddenly to put on hair gel. "Ah, Nathan, is that you? Just two minutes," he said. I also thought of haircuts as clearing space for my third hemisphere so I could sense messages better, but that probably isn't related at all. After that, he made me sit in the chair and draped me in the cover. After my mom told him the hairstyle to do, we began the process. I heard the buzzing of the razor behind my ears, the snipping of the scissors, and the spray of water and gel. At my neck, I had to struggle not to laugh as I felt ticklish. After he blow-dried me, the hair all falling to the ground, he spun me around. Perfect. Now, I looked smart and stylish and could sense messages better. We thanked Wang, paid for the cut, and left. Once we got home, I checked the reply from the district's superintendent:

Reply to “CONFIDENTIAL MATTER” by Kelly Robinson:

It is not safe to talk about this via email. Meet me at the Starbucks on First Street at 5:30, Monday.

Regards,

Kelly Robinson

Superintendent of Livermore Unified School District

Oh, fish! How could I meet her in person, with me being a kid?! By my height, she’d realize I’m just an average middle-schooler who’s probably playing a joke on her. *Unless…* we ask Danny to do it. He was a good size for the job, but would he question what we would ask him to do? I don’t know if I’d consider him *trustworthy*, but hopefully, he has learned from his mistakes of locking horns with Nathan “the Brave” and Ernest “the Valiant” and their great empire of crime-stopping.

The day had finally come when I had convinced my mom to let Noemi and I increase our junk food consumption rate for a day, and so we went to First Street to go to Starbucks. But I wasn't focused on coffee. *I* was focused on getting answers. Entering Starbucks was like entering a haven of coffee. Everywhere you went(even the bathrooms) smelled like coffee. It's like Candy Land but with coffee instead. As my mom was ordering the drinks and snacks, I saw Danny in the corner, his face covered with a surgical mask and a hood. He walked over to the superintendent, who was sitting up straight, wearing sunglasses and a business suit, as if going for a simple negotiation. Danny sat down opposite her and said hoarsely, **"Hand me over the details."** She looked around, then opened up her briefcase. She handed Danny a file, which, by looking at its width, contained at least three hundred pages of paperwork. Dang, we really scared her. Who knew that she was willing to give this much information? "The leader's pen name is "Rey" Rolando, but nobody knows his actual name. According to these details, he made a whole new identity using this name, as the Dexeplin Association was registered as a new pharmaceutical business under his name." It was funny because the word *rey* in Spanish meant "king," implying he was the "king" of the DA. After the very suspicious meeting, Mrs. Robinson left, and Danny handed over the details to me. I thanked him and then gave him ten dollars, a 20% tip for him coping with me and dealing with the dangerous situation. I folded the papers, kept them in my pocket, and left Starbucks with nothing but snacks, coffee, and confidential files.

Recently, I've been too focused on my power, and it has led me to big trouble. I've been too interested in what other people are doing, and so I've been "spying" electronically. Although I was not the guy to spread gossip and that stuff, I do have to admit it was fun looking into what my peers were doing. But I had become too vulnerable and dependent. I realized, when I checked my grades, that I was *missing* an assignment. How could it be? It never happened in middle school(*I was a bit of a procrastinator in elementary school when it came to submitting assignments, but we'll talk about that later*), ever, ever! And it happened now because of my *stupidity*. I had lost my control. My math teacher, Mrs. Gowda, talked to me after class. I said like a military officer, "I will immediately fix the issue, Ma'am!" and added an imaginary salute to the situation in my head, which made me chuckle later. Of course, I had to take action. I completed the assignment but lost ten points for late submission. I hoped that my power would no longer be a diversion to interfere with my work life.

I knew tomorrow I would be visiting my mom's lab, so I asked Ernest to place an anonymous sample testing order on my mom's lab website for Morty's pills. I wanted to know whether the results matched what was on the label. Of course, to avoid suspicion, Ernest transferred the pills to a separate pill bottle, then packed and mailed it to the lab(he made a fake shipping label so no eyebrows would be raised). I knew my mom would sometimes be absent-minded, like me, but she would be exceptionally focused and careful when it came to her job, which was to see the samples and approve their testing. I hope she won't notice when I would go and change the evaluation status of the sample. Knowing tomorrow, I'd find out what exactly happened to Morty made me restless, and I tossed and turned the entire night. It was only four o'clock when I closed my eyes and took a snooze. Great. Less than three hours of sleep. Excellent amount of sleep for a kid your age, Nathan.

Chapter 23

Fun at the Lab

"The true laboratory is the mind, where behind illusions we uncover the laws of truth."

– Jagadish Chandra Bose

After school, I got home, and my mom was there, making us eat a quick snack before we left for her lab. My mom had said, "Nathan, I *should* be punishing you for your late submission, but you know how nice we are about grades." Like this wasn't a punishment, but on the other hand, I needed to come to see the test results of Morty's pills. Noemi and I got board and card games to avoid boredom. When we reached, we saw a small parking space in front of a large lab called Brilliance Biotech Researching. As my mom ushered us to her lab, we had to take some cardboard boxes that had been mailed to her lab. The overall load was heavy, but some boxes were light. We had to make two trips before finally settling in the lab. My mom took us to a place which read in threatening letters:

CAUTION!!

Biohazard! Please wear a mask before entering.

My mom then gave us two oversized, plastic-smelling masks with two eye holes and a circle in the middle for breathing fresh oxygen. My mom said in her mask, "You'll need it," in a slightly amplified voice. With our masks on, we opened the thick titanium door and were amazed by what we saw inside. An entire laboratory of scientists in these masks studying things under microscopes, using automated machines for testing samples. My mom introduced us to some of her colleagues. A guy(who we couldn't really see through the mask) said, "Hey, I'm Jacob. Your mom's told me a lot about you." Noemi and I didn't really know how to respond. We didn't know the guy's last name, and he was older than us, so what should we call him?

"Hey, Jacob," we said in unison.

My mom then showed us the conference room, the break room/cafeteria, the storage room, and other places around her lab. When my mom showed us the room we could be in, we saw another kid there. He was a black-haired, chubby kid younger than us with brown eyes. He waved at us, his eyes lighting up with excitement. "Hi, I'm Dylan. Who are you?" Noemi and I looked at each other. We knew how we found little kids a *teensy* bit annoying and hard to manage. Yet, we introduced ourselves and played our games with him. He was entertaining enough for us to pass the time until the staff and we had to have lunch in the conference room. Dylan was the jester in the conference room. The adults asked us the regular stuff: “What grade are you in?” “How’s middle school?” “What are your hobbies?” “What do you want to be when you grow up?” and all the other formal-yet-trying-to-be-fun-sounding questions. I was the first one to finish eating. My mom gave me a card with the lab’s logo and said, “Scan this card to get in. Go to the cafeteria and throw your trash away. Give me the key after you’re done, ja?” I nodded, then did the needful. I realized that the messages I intercepted here were either personal messages or business messages(surprisingly, the amount of business messages was less than the personal messages). After washing my hands, I returned and sat down to wait for everyone else to finish eating. After everybody finished, my mom allowed us to use her computer in her office under the condition that we took equal turns. When it was my turn, I let Dylan play on the computer and told him I was going to use the restroom. Instead, I went into the room where they kept the online record of each sample. I took my glasses out of my pocket and then logged onto my mom's computer. I had looked at the password she used to sign in to her computer at home, so I assumed the code was the same. I successfully logged in, peered from above my glasses to make sure the coast was clear and then opened up the app. Hundreds of samples organized by the date received were in the spreadsheet. Thankfully, I managed to recognize the way it was sorted. Otherwise, I never would have located Morty's pills, which were amongst the topmost in the spreadsheet. I looked at the door once again, my heart thumping like a raccoon trapped in a box. I replaced the evaluation status from "Pending" to "Processing Ready." This would help speed up the process. Luckily, I didn't have to come back to the lab after a few days to get the sample results back. They were sent via email, and this online method made my job much easier. When I returned to the room, Dylan had a set of cards in his hand and two small piles of cards in the other. "Want to play Crazy 8s? Oh, don’t worry, I didn’t even take a peak.” he squeaked innocently. Noemi and I looked at each other, shrugged, and went to join the game. I looked at my watch. 4:46. We’d be leaving in about an hour. It wouldn't hurt to play *a little more* with Dylan. “By the way, which of your parents works around here?” Noemi inquired. “None,” Dylan said blankly as he slapped down a seven of diamonds. “My dad died in an accident, and my mom died due to a drug overdose. I live with my brother, Jacob.” he sighed. Oh, so Jacob was Dylan’s brother. But it was so sad what they had to go through. I couldn’t imagine living without my parents, but it would save me from going bananas in doubt and hesitation. My family was first on my protection list(if I called it a “caring list,” it wouldn’t suit me). If I had to choose between saving family or friends, I would try to save both(unless I could only choose one, then it would be family). I patted Dylan on the back. “Hey, I’m sure Jacob will take good care of you.” I consoled him as his eyes layered with tears. My mind kept going back to what happened to his mom. A drug overdose. It was becoming so common. Morty, Dylan's mom, and who knows? It could keep happening to anyone, and even our near and dear ones. Noemi won the game, slamming down her last card and cocking a sly grin at us. "Good game," I said and shook her hand. Soon, my mom entered our room and said, "Guys, time to go. *Bye*, Dylan." my mom waved with a smile. Well, a day in my mom's lab, not bad. Not bad at all.

Chapter 24

Dodging Suspicion

"Avoiding danger is no safer in the long run than outright exposure. The fearful are often caught as the bold."

– Helen Keller

Over the course of this week, I have ensured that the tables don't turn and that fingers don't point at me. Remember, I mentioned that I was allowing my ability to take control of me, and I was focusing too much on what other people were doing(A.K.A. snooping)? Well, other than missing an assignment, it ended up sprouting a *much* bigger issue. Let me tell you what happened in this week of dodging suspicion.

Monday: It was the start of a normal, boring school week with never-ending assignments, lectures, and troubles. However, in Mrs. Gowda's class, tension started to arise. I overheard a group of kids discussing something related to their phones.

"Hey guys, this is really creepy, but I think there's a hacker."

"Same, bro. People start to know things before I do."

"Yeah, like yesterday, I got my grade on the quiz, and some dudes told me they already knew my score. Gotta be careful these days."

"Are you all talking about a hacker?" Mrs. Gowda intervened. The trio nodded. "We've been noticing our info being leaked," said Matt, a tall and burly kid with an Adidas T-shirt, jeans, and Nike shoes. "Me too. I was going shopping one day, and my friends came to know. They started to shop with me, though I'd much rather prefer shopping in solitude. I had messaged my other contacts that I would be out shopping, but they had never met my friends before." Mrs. Gowda sighed, then shook her head in unease. She then announced, "Class, today we will move on to our data and statistics unit. Camille, please pass out these packets." But the new unit was of least concern. The trio that was allegedly being hacked squinted at each student with suspicion. I hope this mess didn't land on me. I may have blabbed something to people about other people's plans based on their messaging. The rest of Monday went pretty well, and the topic wasn't brought up ever after. But on Tuesday, the revolution was *really* starting to cook. A group of students under the impression of being hacked formed a community called "*The Online Information Protection Society,*" or TOIPS. Their goal, in simple terms, was to find out who the hacker or hackers were and confront them. The whole of Tuesday was nerve-racking, as I held an uncomfortable, neutral expression as they squinted at everybody, their trust in no one but amongst themselves. For a moment, I put myself in their shoes. If I didn't have my ability, I certainly would feel threatened if a hacker was snooping on what I did. But how were they so sure it was a student who was doing all this? I had to inform Ernest as well, so the blame doesn't fall on him for his tech skills. I made sure to be extra cautious about what I said; otherwise, I'd accidentally tell somebody about another person's plan, and then the fault would be mine. Sheesh. To peacefully sleep that night, I had told myself to keep a poker face in my belt, for if I needed it, I was obligated to use it.

In the middle of the week, Wednesday, I decided to be the rat and gnaw at it. I didn't know if the plan would work out or not, but I decided to give it a shot. I claimed I was facing information leaks too, and dramatically declared, "WE MUST PUT AN END TO THIS OPPRESSION!" with a raised fist. The rat was in. I successfully joined TOIPS, and now I needed to execute a second job, which could have taken a day or several months. I *needed* to break the group from the inside out. It seemed like an evil thing to do, but security is most important for text message interceptors. The TOIPS idea was good, I'll admit, but I'd rather have it recreated sometime later and far away from me. Thursday: The day with a win, then a loss. I had poured the acid, and now it was dissolving. I managed to convince Matt and the other people who created TOIPS that it was simply paranoia and that the likelihood of a hacker within the school itself was very low. I told them to simply install some strong online virus and tracker protections on their devices, and they would be fine. They took my advice into consideration, and on December 14, 2018, *The Online Information Protection Society* officially collapsed. Historical moment. I then finished the school day with a headache gone and peace of mind. But mistakes happen. I had only realized it on Friday when the former members of TOIPS re-created it due to another info spread. Matt and the co-founders of TOIPS hosted a small get-together at his house, and some uninvited guests showed up at the party. The problem not only arose once again, but it rose in *the wrong place*. I realized my *stupidity* and absent-mindedness had led me to break the news to a few people from the group. I had to get this out of the way; otherwise, it could be a big pain later on. If people stopped sending messages, my contribution to the community(good or bad) wouldn’t be as significant. If one has to believe there is a purpose for everything, then my ability also does have a purpose. Sitting on it would be an option if I have a way to turn it off at will. But I can’t, hence the actions I caused. I half-hoped that Matt didn't install the privacy software just yet. Then I could prove my argument and stop this from escalating. As all political leaders know, if a conflict arises that opposes you, the only way to prevent it from growing is to *destroy* it. “Hey guys, let’s chill out for a sec, explore the facts,” I announced. “Matt, did you have everybody get the security extensions?” He nodded. I gulped. “Did you add it to all of your browsers and apps?” He shook his head. I felt relief wash over me. “See? We must be thorough in our work. Now, the person who *dared* to hack us won’t be able to. I believe I talked to you guys earlier about how unlikely it is for a hacker to be in our school, too. I think we shouldn't let this get to our heads, and maybe we are exaggerating the situation. When you send a message, the receiver can send it to another person, and it continues." The society seemed convinced now. Nathan and his charisma. "I agree with Nate, ain't got no people to hate, just gotta sit back and wait, Nate, Nate." Bill, my tablemate and rap artist, sang. I pointed to him and gave him a polite round of applause, although nobody joined me. I realized my charm fades away so quickly. Bummer.

I watched from my bedroom window as I saw an ocean-colored sedan parked near my neighbor's house. I had seen this car before. It had made frequent visits to my neighbor's house. The Horlick family lived there, polished, classy Brits who had hosted many events in their house. Mr. Horlick was a retired businessman who handed his company to Easton Horlick, his son. Mr. Horlick had moved here long before we did and ensured his son would get an American education and expand his business. But these sus visits were random and occurred with no specific pattern. I was confused about who to suspect: my neighbors or the driver of this vehicle? I was kind of an insomniac, as I wouldn't get sleep immediately. I would have to go through a long book or stay awake until midnight to get some sleep. I was determined to continue to monitor the suspicious activity later on. Today, I happened to catch a glimpse of the driver. He exited the vehicle with a black briefcase and an expensive gray suit. I sighed. I was going crazy. I shouldn't have worried so much. Easton Horlick exited the car and unlocked his house doors. I shouldn't suspect every weird, out-of-place thing going on! I should simply suspect what was related to my problems, which was drug manufacturing. And wouldn't you know it, right next to me on my bed were *The Mysterious Case of Dr. Jekyll and Mr. Hyde* and *The Hound of the Baskervilles*, two mystery classics I hadn't read yet? There were other mystery novels I had, but I had recently borrowed these from the library so I could add them to my checklist. When I see teachers behaving dubiously about something, and I notice more shady meetings and deals being done, I can always just use my inner text message reader and see what's going on. Easy-peasy. *These* were the things to doubt, not a mysterious car parked in front of my neighbor's house that *actually* belonged to my neighbor. *Focus on what's related*, I told myself. With a tool in my head that can sniff out the most suspicious messages, I simply had to improve it and solve the big drug dealer mystery. Who knew that this week would not only be dodging suspicion but also having suspicion?

Chapter 25

An Accidental Discovery

"Great discoveries are made accidentally less often than the populace likes to think."

– Wilhelm Röntgen

My school was canceled today due to an inclement weather day. There was nothing to do since I had finished all of my homework and submitted it. So, I helped my dad in cleaning out the attic. Our attic was a dusty place with loose floorboards, Amazon boxes towering over our heads like skyscrapers in New York, and was the place with the most heat in all of the house. Each box had a different set of items, all belonging to the same theme. For example, one of the boxes had old clothes, another one of them had old books and photo albums, and one had toys previously belonging to Noah. *That* box particularly interested me as my dad began to separate the gadgets into piles. Whenever we cleaned out our belongings, we would always sort them into piles of three different categories: donation, throw-away, and keep. We typically would donate our old clothes, toys, books, and electronic devices to Goodwill or the church nearby. If one of the items was in no condition to be kept or to be donated, then we would simply recycle it(depending on what it was). The "keep" pile had the least amount of items, as we only kept what was necessary and minimized most things. There was one exception to these three main categories: selling. From whatever I could recall, I could only remember one time when my dad had sold some of his vintage He-Man action figures on Craigslist. My dad pulled out something from the box that brought back a wave of memories and cravings. Noah's favorite toy. There it was, the legendary remote-controlled convertible car. It was red as a ruby, a color that reminded me of my mom's nail polish. As a young kid, I remembered its power as it zoomed through the house, little

Noah waddling around behind it. I had so desperately wanted it, but Noah wasn't willing to share. Both of us were young and stubborn at the time, and as we grew, we quickly forgot about it. The remote had started to dysfunction, my six-year-old self watching sorrowfully as twelve-year-old Noah tossed it into a box and kept it in the attic. But now that I had found it, the glory, the power, it was all *mine* now. I ran downstairs to ask my mom if I could borrow her phone so I could text Noah. She accepted my request delightfully, as she always liked her children interacting well with each other. I found Noah's contact from my mother's never-ending list. I took a photo of the old car and sent it to him. I then typed:

Hey, it's Nathan. Found your remote-controlled car while cleaning out the attic. I'm gonna use it.

I then switched off the phone since my ability would let me see Noah's response. Judging by the amount of time it took Noah to respond, I could tell he still felt a little insecure with the car in my hands.

Noah:

Go enjoy yourself. The old thing doesn't even work. [U+1F60F]

He gave me the smirk emoji. Although he was a man with proper behavior and all, this proved he had a small amount of childishness left in him.

We'll see about that. I typed back.

I had found some entertainment. I would install new batteries to the remote and the car and play around with it. Of course, to exasperate Noah, I would film myself playing with the car. I slowly sneaked out of the attic before Dad could notice. I opened the battery case and found it filled with white powder, its odor putrid and unpleasant. I quickly threw the tarnished thing away. I then went to search for a battery, the car and remote jiggling around in my pocket as I walked. After a thorough inspection, I couldn't find what I was looking for. Just when I was about to lose hope, I saw my mom taking her car keys and wearing her shoes. Just before she opened the door, I shouted, "Mom, where are you going?" She stopped and said, "Oh, just running a few errands to Costco and Albertsons. Want to come with me?" I nodded my head vigorously. She grinned and said, "My my, Nathan, I've never seen you this eager to go anywhere." I shrugged. "I'm feeling kind of bored sitting around at home." I put on a pair of sneakers as Mom gleefully rushed to the car. As I sat in the front seat, she quickly glanced through her shopping list, which she always had ready on her phone. She started the car, it growling to life. We reached pretty fast because of the empty roads; my mom had chosen a good time to shop. My family and I go to Costco every Saturday, which excites me because Costco is my favorite store. You might be wondering, "*Why does an average middle-school kid with superpowers find entertainment in going to a superstore?*" Well, my main reason is the books. Costco has an *amazing, innumerable* amount of books, especially books that kids of my age would like. While my family goes shopping in the other departments, I would spend my entire time there reading and checking out books. I had an entire collection of books at home, and 90% of those were from Costco. My favorite genres were historical fiction, science fiction, specific fantasy novels, nonfiction texts, and crime/mystery, especially classics. You may have noticed how I'm overly cautious and paranoid; that's due to the crime novels. My second reason, the food. My mom, being the best cook in the world, bought most of her ingredients from Costco. Since I've been brought up with her food, of course, I love it, and it's all thanks to Costco. Dang, if I told the CEO of Costco this, I would be on TV, and my words would be quoted on billboards all across Livermore. But that *wasn't* going to happen anytime soon. I need to keep low and be undercover. If I become famous and I have this uncontrollable ability, then I could get bad. But anyway, after Costco, I liked Aldi's, Walmart, Albertsons, and Whole Foods.

Today, Costco's parking lot has countless amount of spaces for us to park, contrary to the packed parking lot on weekends. My mom asked me to pull out a shopping cart and give it to her. I asked her if I could go see the latest books that had come out. She agreed and told me she'd stop by there to pick me up when we left. I started to look at the books, my mom migrating to another area in the superstore. I then tried to go find the batteries, careful not to run into my mom. I also needed to search quickly; otherwise, my mom would freak out if I wasn't near the book section. I ran from aisle to aisle in search of batteries and finally stumbled upon them. Each of the batteries was either cylindrical, block-like, and thick or thin. Judging by the space within the miniature car's battery holder, what I needed was a thick cuboid battery, typically a 9V. I foraged through the rack of batteries but couldn't obtain the exact battery of my liking. I didn't think there would be any other place in Costco with this type of battery, so I rushed back towards the book section and skimmed through the latest releases. My mom found me as I was looking through *Tom Sawyer and Huckleberry Finn* by Mark Twain, books I had already read, but in an adapted, more simplified version. "Okay, Nathan, time to go to Albertsons." my mom called me as I flipped through the rest of the book, then sauntered alongside her. We set our purchases on the slider machine and watched as our items were brought closer to the cashier, then scanned and dropped into our cart, the cashier showing her expertise in her fluid scanning motion. "That'll be seventy-two, ninety-eight, ma'am." My mom inserted her card into the credit card machine and then took it out. After we exited the building, we filled the trunk with our things and headed toward Albertsons. Knowing

Costco as a resourceful, abundant place, I was beginning to feel unsure about what I would get at Albertsons. I didn't know what I would tell my mom because there were no books in Albertsons, and there was nowhere I could ask her if I could stay. With utter dissatisfaction, I trudged through the store until my eyes fell on something. A fluffy, gray-colored recliner was on sale in one of the aisles. That was it! "Hey, Mom, I'm going to go check out that recliner." She took a look at it, and even she was immediately fascinated by it. "Okay, Nathan, check it out and tell me how it feels; I'll meet you back here when I'm done shopping." I gave her a thumbs-up and waited for her to leave. I then followed the same procedure I did at Costco, searching the entire store for a simple 9V battery. It seemed quite stupid and arrogant; all this physical activity and sneakiness for reviving an old toy car that once belonged to my elder brother, just to annoy him. I shook my head. I finally found a shelf of blue batteries, shapes similar to the ones at Costco. After raiding the shelf, I found what I was looking for. The box-shaped, 9V battery. I held it in my hands with triumph for a dramatic moment, then rushed back to the spot where the recliner was being sold. Whew. Mom wasn't there. After relaxing for some time in the fuzzy, soft lounge chair, I saw my mom come by with a cart loaded with food, dairy, and beauty products. Perfect. I got up, greeted my mom, and dropped the pack of batteries without my mom noticing. "So, how's the recliner?" she asked me. I couldn't really say it was okay to purchase, as I only sampled it for a minute. "I didn't think it had the right vibe for our house. And besides, we need Dad to help bring it back home." I said, supplying different points to tell my mom I didn't like it. "Okay, then, let's go home," she concluded. When we got to the check-out area, my mom was puzzled as to what a packet of batteries was doing in her cart. She made a "so-what" face, then put it on the conveyor belt. The jugs of milk wobbled as they moved on the conveyor, then were scanned and placed into our cart. We paid for the items, thanked the cashier, and left Albertsons. Mission: Battery was successful.

At home, I put the battery holders of both the car and the remote on our dining table, then went to retrieve the newly bought pair of batteries. I ripped open the packet and pulled out two batteries clutched tightly in my hand. As I was about to place them in their respective containers, a sudden jolt came through me. I was able to intercept hundreds, maybe thousands of messages, all whizzing through my head at the speed of light. I immediately dropped the battery on the table, causing it to thud loudly. “Nathan, all okay?” My mom inquired from afar. “Yup,” I replied. I was startled but amazed at what I had stumbled upon. I’d have to inform Ernest afterward about my discovery. Well, my *accidental* discovery. To be able to avoid the avalanche of messages, I found out that I had to hold the battery from its midsection instead of top and bottom. To control the flow of messages, I gripped it in a particular way, where my index fingers of both hands held the charge points, and my thumbs held the base. I wrote this down in the logbook Ernest, and I looked after. Since we didn't meet very frequently, we also kept a digital copy of our theories and discoveries. I'll have to update that document soon. I finally was able to place the batteries in their holders and got the remote and car to function properly once again. I sent a video of me controlling the car to Noah, the property now working under my authority. Noah later sent a gif of someone rolling their eyes. I chuckled, then sent him a shrug emoji. Well, it looked like a foolish quest for bringing a toy convertible to work again, resulting in an amazing discovery. I couldn't even perceive the power of my ability if I had batteries in both my hands. I could intercept so many messages, and I could help so many people. Or wreak *havoc*.

Ernest shared his screen on the video call after he received the email regarding the sample results. This meant my mom genuinely hadn't regarded the small change I made to the records. She probably got too many samples that day to notice. When we compared the results of the test to what was on the label, our eyes widened. The potency percentages were twice what was written on the label. It was the same amount of pills and the same dosage, but different ingredient amounts being reported. So many questions were already answered, and so many more questions and their answers would follow. Morty had died, not because he was taking the pills too much, but because the amount of the drug was so high. Eventually, his body reacted to the stopping of the medication. I sighed with sorrow. Now we knew what crime the Dexeplin Association was hiding. All this smaller evidence was now more significant than what it was initially. All this evidence now had *meaning*. The revenge for Morty now had *direction*. It was time to sharpen our weapons. The eve of battle would be arriving soon.

Chapter 26

El Rey (The King)

"Time's glory is to calm contending kings, To unmask falsehood, and to bring truth to light."

–William Shakespeare

We called over some of our close family friends, friends my father and mother had known before Noah was even born. "Hi, Seema and Rahul, come on in!" said my dad enthusiastically as my dad hugged Rahul and my mom hugged Seema. Rahul Uncle was my dad's best buddy from childhood days in India, and after that, my dad went to North Carolina and Rahul to San Francisco. Then, when Rahul Uncle found out that my dad had moved to

California, they had once-in-a-while visits, so they got to see my siblings and me as we grew. "Nathan, how are you doing?" Seema Auntie said as she hugged me. Rahul Uncle shook my hand, patted me on my back, and then started the usual adult conversation. It was kind of an Indian thing to call the guests by respectful names, like saying their real name, then add an Uncle *ji* or Auntie *ji*. The good thing was they had kids my age: twins, a boy(Roshan) and a girl(Vidya). Roshan and I would play video games(of course, the only time I ever played video games was with other kids because *they* had no other form of entertainment for themselves) and chat, while Noemi and Vidya, well, I don't know what they did together. I never interfered in their business. After Roshan and I squared off in *Arsenal* and a game called *Cinema Scrimmage 3D*, we had to come down for dinner. There, my mom served us fluffy naan with steaming paneer, along with a German dish called currywurst. Everyone knew how well my mom cooked, so as soon as the food was put on the plate, they began to gobble it, their esophagi not having enough time to react to the immediate swallowing of food. After serving everyone, my mom sat herself down and began eating. The men enjoyed their mugs of beer while the ladies tinked their cups of wine. The kids were served coke, and all was going splendidly until the excellent, mouth-watering paneer had a troublesome lizard in it. It had probably fallen from the ceiling. Noemi and Vidya shrieked. The ladies gasped. My dad and Rahul Uncle, oblivious to what was happening, were busy with their chatter and drinks. I had to take the lead. I dashed to get a broom and dustpan. I saw the lizard scurrying along the table, leaving behind tiny orange footprints from the paneer gravy. I put the tray under the table, then scooped the pest into the dustpan and trapped it with my broom. Then I asked my mom to open the front door and flung the critter outside. I slammed the front door shut, tired of chasing the reptile. Everyone was overwhelmed, but clapped at my immediate reaction to the problem. I hid my inner smile of pride and basked in the glory. Of course, *nobody* would eat the paneer now, but the rest of the dinner went well. After dinner, we spent some more time talking and playing, and then they left. Well, so much for *dinner*.

Today, my science teacher, Mr. Nuñez, wasted 30 minutes explaining about the science fair. He said, and I quote, “It’s for your benefit,” and, “You’ll have so much fun doing these projects.” Look, Sir, I have wasted my time in elementary school making project after project and not getting first place. My topics were complicated, above my level, and interesting, yet the judges chose something like “How To Make A Volcano” or something a kindergartener made(usually “Sink or Float” or “Can Pigs Fly?”). They required so much work, and yet I only got a participation award! So, this year, I decided to screw it. I am in middle school, and there are already a lot of assignments; plus, I have a superpower, so *no thank you*. If I was going to do the science fair this year, it would have been titled, “Do Humans Really

Need Messaging Platforms?” This would be an easy subject to present for a person with my power, but I just needed to substitute it with the science aspect. Maybe the judges would find my project “top-three worthy.” I had gotten a third-place award in third grade for explaining the increase of myopia, or nearsightedness, in children. Instead of just leaving it in the room for people to come and inspect(which nobody did at the age of eight), this time, I decided to present it to the class. My class was staring at me like I was speaking a different language when I talked about the basic information and stats, a diagram of the normal eye and myopic eye, and the process of reaching nearsightedness. My third-grade science teacher, Ms. Argent, was more engaged in my information, probably because she suffered from it herself(she never told the class she had myopia, but it was evident from the thick glasses frame she used to wear). After I showed the many treatment options and gave a conclusion to support my hypothesis, the class clapped very unenthusiastically. Even after my presentation, a good chunk of my class who had stayed with me in the grade levels following third grade still had glasses. It was no use, no use at all.

Recently, we were learning about the periodic table and its organizational structure in science class. I've always been a big fan of chemistry, as well as classifying things. If things weren't classified, we wouldn't know what to call it, hence why I like classification in any discipline. I liked how the periodic table was organized, keeping all elements with similar properties and uses together. Another reason why I liked the periodic table was the names of elements. They were named after people, places, mythological figures, etc. Some of my favorite elements, either based on their strange name, importance in the world, or mythology, are yttrium, titanium, magnesium, hydrogen, carbon, oxygen, nitrogen, promethium, uranium, neptunium, plutonium, etc. I also found the elements that had symbols based on their Latin name very interesting, like gold, silver, iron, mercury, lead, and more. These were just because of their names. I would see certain combustion reactions, cool colors from diffusions, and other videos that would educate me on higher-level chemistry concepts that would get me through my science education. This included physics, biology, and other subjects. Once, during science class, Mr. Nuñez gave us all a "Periodic Table of Elements" word search. I don't know why somebody made that word search in the first place; all you had to do was find "-ium" and then the small percentage of the elements without "-ium." I was able to finish it within 15 minutes, which surprisingly shocked my science teacher. "Good job, Nathan. It looks like your interest in pursuing chemistry has fueled your quick solution to this challenging puzzle." *Challenging*? I was amused. I got to spend the rest of the day doing free time, which increased the jealousy of the class.

Ernest had a theory that at any point in my life, I could have come in contact with one of these elements, which triggered my power. In his list of possibilities, this was the lowest, but hey, the whole point of a *possibility* was that it was somehow *possible*.

Mrs. Cabrera, my Spanish teacher, was a brunette with red pointed spectacles. She would never *ever* come to school without her precious heels, which seemed to be taller than the size of her legs. She paced around the classroom, collected our daily warm-ups, and returned to her desk. She told us we would be starting Unit 4, but looking at the lesson plan, Pablo had taken me to Unit 12 already. Some of the kids who already knew Spanish took this time to have an afternoon nap, dozing through class, yet still make a 100 on every assignment. "Hello, class," she said, neatly organizing her papers and putting them in a drawer. "Today is the start of Unit

4, and by the end of the school year, you will learn basic Spanish speaking skills. Go ahead and copy the vocabulary words for Lesson 1." I quickly wrote them down, then yawned. Of course, this class period's time was spent in boredom-relieving activities, like solving a Rubik's cube or doodling. "Okay, I have given you enough time to write the words; now it's time to say them and put them in sentences." I interpreted this class as language arts but in a different language. The concept was the same. "Vamos al museo," Mrs. Cabrera announced. "VAMOS AL MUSEO," the class said monotonously. "And can anybody tell me what that means?" My hand shot up in the air. "Ooh, Nathan looks like he wants to volunteer. Tell me, Nathan."

I said, "It means 'Let's go to the museum.'" "Good job!" Mrs. Cabrera exclaimed and high-fived me. Some chatter was going on between Lucas, Mateo, and Adrián, so the teacher quietly walked over to their desk and whispered, "*No es cortés hablar durante la clase,*" which translated to “It’s not polite to talk during the class.” See, now I’m a Spanish whiz! I was really thankful to Pablo, not only for helping me ace my Spanish class but also for helping me understand any Spanish messages being sent. After finishing more notes and activities, the bell rang, and it was time to finally get back home. Wait, I had to stay back at school because I had my orchestra concert at six. It’s funny that I completely forgot why I was wearing a fancy suit and tie.

It was time for my orchestra concert. The colorful lights shined brightly on the violin, viola, cello, and bass players. Mr. Tarou was standing in the front, directing his students, with his always serious face. He turned to the audience and announced, “Welcome to the Spring Beginners’ Orchestra Concert! Today, your talented kids will display to you their newly learned expertise in fine-stringed instruments. As you can see, they are all focused on me and prepared for this concert. Give them a round of applause for their hard work!" The auditorium was filled with intense clapping, especially from joyful parents who were in tears. "Now, the first song is from a movie series that parents in here have seen as kids and still like to watch with family." Mr. Tarou raised his hands, and the strings began to play the harmonies of the *Star Wars* theme song. The violins and violas played the mellower, higher tones, and the cellos and basses played deeper, lower tones. The size of the instruments seemed to reflect how they sound, as per Mr. Tarou's lecture. After the song was over, there was another round of applause. "The next song is a piece meant to be expressed using classical string instruments, as well as the piano. We have called this amazing professional pianist, Mr. Yakov Kaminski, for the accompaniment." Mr. Tarou lifted his hands. The pianist started playing, every note sounding unique to me. I was lost in the playing of the piano, the arpeggios, the scales, the intricate and detailed playing. It all seemed like the music *itself* was designed for such an instrument. I was so deep in the music I hadn't even realized we had started playing. The person sitting next to me nudged me with his leg, and I started playing. Mr. Tarou gave me a scowl. I had even played a couple of wrong notes in the song, getting an even nastier scowl each time I had done so. After the piece was done, Mr. Tarou stated, his tone hot, "Pardon the minor mistakes. Just some students who didn't *practice enough*." He turned back to glare at me. He mouthed, "*You should be thankful for that.*" He turned back. I gulped. This concert was a major grade in orchestra. If I get below an 80 on this, then I'll try band classes. Or choir. Be a "la-la loser" for a little while. In sixth grade, the names for people in orchestra, band, or choir were "orch dorks," "band kids," and "la-la losers," respectively. The orchestra and choir kids had found it very appalling that the students in the band were just "band kids."

Ben, a choir kid, had found a new classification for the people in the band. “The band bums!” he had announced proudly that day at my lunch table. “And now, the grand finale, from the Disney movie Coco.” The violins, violas, cellos, and basses started to play *Remember Me*. The auditorium was resonating with mesmerizing melodies and heavenly harmonies. After the concert, my dad, having observed my poor performance, gave an evaluation. “Nathan, to be *frank*, I don’t think you are interested in learning the violin.” My mom nodded in agreement. “Would you like to learn another instrument?” I thought about it for a little while, and then it struck me. The piano. I *really* wanted to learn the piano. “I would like to take piano lessons,” I confessed to my parents. “We can do that for you, Nathan, but you can’t learn piano at school, can you?” The piano, among other instruments, was not an instrument that you could learn in my middle school. “There are only a few months remaining until summer break, so I think I’ll stay in orchestra. But please don’t expect me to get good grades in it." I stated, coming to a final decision. My parents also thought this was a good idea, and the rest of the day went well. I knew if I listened and practiced piano, it would serve as a remedy to any strenuous activity, whether it be physical or related to my third hemisphere.

There are an infinite amount of problems in a middle school's cafeteria, but there are two main ones: the crowd, and the constant food fight attempts. When it was my first day at Livermore Middle School, I was appalled by the amount of people. By the time you get to the end of the lunch line, the bell has already rung, and you have to go to the next class. So, my mom just makes lunch for me, which is honestly better than having greasy, smelly pizzas and spoilt french fries and mashed potatoes. Number two: Food fight attempts. Previously, the school's safety prohibitions weren't as strong, so food fights were common occurrences. Now, when people see apple baseballs and pizza boomerangs thrown across the cafeteria, the teachers usually suspend the person, or people, temporarily. For the rare times ketchup landed on my face or clothes, my mom had spare clothes packed. Gee, I owe my mom *a lot*. Today, the cafeteria seemed unusually quiet, and I finally realized why. Our assistant principal, Ms. Dominus, had to do lunch duty for an absent teacher. She paced around each table, asking everyone what they brought for lunch, and said she should try it out. I had brought two taquitos with sour cream and guacamole in two compartments of my lunch box. Ms. Dominus said, 'Nathan, right? That's some tasty-looking taquitos right there. Did your mom make it?' I nodded. Ms. Dominus then addressed all the people at my table. 'Anybody happen to find anything about SpectersCloak23?' Everyone stared at each other, and then Ryan, a blond, athletic kid with a tendency to be very 'hands-on', said 'Nope.' She nodded in pensive thinking, then gave us a bright smile. 'Well, then, you gentlemen can carry on with your day. No getting in trouble, though; I don't want to see you guys again today. Just kidding.' We smiled back at her, and continued our lunch. It was so fortunate that there was a teacher like Ms. Dominus to have our back. Who knew middle school was capable of having such a sympathetic and fun teacher?

I had been listening to some piano songs, especially those of J.S. Bach, Beethoven, and Chopin. My parents had already bought me a Roland FP-25 electric piano from Costco(thankfully, it was on discount; otherwise, they probably wouldn’t have bought it). I looked at some online videos for basic piano and quickly advanced along the way. Then, I again used my online resources to learn how to read music. My newfound interest and a new place to spend time overjoyed my parents. As I listened to *Sonate*,

Op. 49, No.2 by Beethoven, on my headphones, I got a new message.

Kelly Robinson:

2-17-8 47-4-10 177-9-6 34-6-1 68-2-9 291-4-2 99-3-5 128-2-1 59-9-4 32-6-1 225-3-9. 202-17-8 48-2-6.

Rey:

202-17-8 43-8-4 283-7-7 39-1-5 190-3-6 19-1-9 239-5-8!!!!

It *had* to be one of them near my house, either Mrs. Robinson or the Rey Rolando dude who controls the DA. I could feel how easy it was to get these messages, unlike the ones that were sent from afar. I rushed outside, heart thumping, to get a glance at the individual we were conspiring against. Not a sign of him. Only a red convertible from the 70s, the person driving whistling a tune. A pipe was held in the hand that wasn't driving, a trail of smoke both from the car and the pipe following behind. And, of course, the hand glinted from the light shining off the signet ring of the Dexeplin Association. Even though I couldn't see him, I could tell he was old-fashioned, the car, pipe, and all that. The code they were using was being tackled by Ernest and me, but I could tell Rey Rolando was angry because of the emojis he used(the devil-angry emoji and the cursing emoji). I wrote down the message so I could jot down the time, date, and message in the notebook Ernest was keeping track of. Hopefully, we will tackle the code soon. Hopefully.

"Let's see, we know that Coach Vencer, the principal, the superintendent, and Ibrahim Ayyad are involved in this…" Ernest stated, obviously trying to find another clue using logical reasoning. "Gee, I don't know, Nathan, I can't find how to connect the dots." I nodded, thinking. "In this whole ordeal, one person we forgot to deal with is the coach," I said.

"Yeah, *so*?"

"Well, I think he might have more importance than we thought," I said, wearing my glasses and opening up Google on my computer. "I believe he was the one who developed this messaging code for the DA."

"How do you know that?" Ernest asked, not sure where I was going with this conclusion.

"You how he keeps ranting on about winning at all costs during PE? Well, let's search it up."

I typed in "win at all costs" in the browser, and we found many results related to the book "Win at All Costs: Inside Nike Running and Its Culture of Deception." We searched through the electronic copy of the book and found many results relating to performance-enhancing drugs. We slowly turned our heads to look at each other, drawing the same conclusion.

"So the code they use in the messaging is from *this book!?*"

Ernest gasped in disbelief, the first one to speak it aloud.

"Well, there's only one way to find out," I said slyly. "Get out the record book of my previous messages, and let's see if we can decode them."

"Man, this is gonna be so much fun."

128-15-3 39-12-5 54-2-9 94-6-5 71-4-7 OWSSRTL OEEKLPZ, * 0 97-5-10.

"The page is 128, and it's the fifteenth word," I said, pointing to the messy handwriting. We tried many different ways the numbers would translate into letters but didn't find anything. Ernest then suggested that the cipher could have a page number-line number-word number format. After deciphering the code using the new idea and substituting the letters, our result was, "We need to meet. Crimson Comedor, 8 o'clock."

"WE DID IT!!!" Ernest shrieked dramatically, which probably was too much of an overreaction. But hey, we cracked a code that a group involved in illegal prescription misprints was using. So, sure, that kind of reaction was okay in such a situation. Ernest dashed out of the room and came with a bottle of chilled Bundaberg ginger ale. He raised the glass, snapped it open, then exclaimed, "Cheers to cracking the code!"

"Cheers."

Our glasses clashed violently, grateful that nothing spilled(then my mom would probably be fuming, and I'd have to spend my time drying it up.) As we were sipping the ginger ale, I asked Ernest to record the new message I got. We decoded it and wrote out the newly translated message.

KELLY ROBINSON:

I WAS FORCED TO SHARE SOME MINOR DETAILS ABOUT THE DA. I APOLOGIZE.

REY:

😼😬I AM VERY DISAPPOINTED IN YOUR INCOMPETENCE!!!...

It looked like Rey currently wasn't on good terms with Mrs. Robinson for her, quote, "incompetence," unquote. We could use this to our advantage. I grabbed a pencil as I felt a message come.

Rey:

29-16-4 40-13-6 55-3-8 95-7-4 72-5-8 25-2-4 5-6-7 30-15-3 58-7-3 48-1-9 101-2-6,) 98-4-9.

When translating numbers, we realized that the use of numbers came from the symbols above the numbers on the keyboard. The message translated to "Meet me at the new real estate sale on Fourth St., 10 P.M."

I asked, "Ernest, we *might* have to sneak out of our houses to stop by for a visit to the DA's meeting area."

Ernest scoffed. "What do you mean, 'stop by for a *visit*'?! We'll get into bigger trouble than you think!"

I stared at him, my expression unmoved.

"*Fine*." he sighed. "Just leave before something happens."

I waited for Ernest's signal as the clock struck 9:30. I peered outside my window, and there he was, Ernest flashing his bike lights. I sneaked downstairs, slowly took my bike out, and joined Ernest in a nighttime ride. Ernest had the directions up on his phone, so I followed him. We saw the street sign of Fourth Street, and right under that, there was a smaller sign saying "**ESTATE SALE**." This *had* to be it. We turned and only stopped when the monotonous, boring directions voice groused, "***You have reached your destination.***" We parked our bikes and peered into the window of the house where criminals would be meeting soon. Many cars were parked in front of the house; some faces known, such as the principal, superintendent, Mr. Ayyad, and some unknown. The living room was organized with two sofas facing each other and a single seat that overlooked the sofas. Everyone managed to fit in the sofas, but no one *dared* to sit in the single seat. I could guess why. Everyone waited in eerie silence. Suddenly, a sharp, beastly shrill echoed in the darkness. The silhouette of a man darkened the living room. The man seemed to be wearing a crown and held a king's orb. This had to be him. Rey Rolando. Everyone got up at once, greeting their leader with respect.

"Greetings, all may be seated."

His deep, authoritative voice sounded foreign, yet I could sense some familiarity. Everyone we suspected was sitting on the couch, proving that it was not somebody *we knew* was in the DA.

"We have come to know that *someone* wishes to damage our well-organized pharmaceutical system, all thanks to *Mrs. Robinson*."

He was wearing a mask, so I couldn't tell if he was glaring. Mrs. Robinson looked down in shame. "Therefore, I have informed the officials, and they vowed to arrest the individual trying to destroy our perfect organization. In case the other possibility happens, and we become at fault for mislabeling our drugs, then before *we* are thrown in jail, I will give you, as the most loyal of all who are involved, my identity."

My heart thumped loudly. He removed his idiotic crown, set it on a nearby table, then removed his mask. I sucked in a deep breath. This was the dramatic moment, which should've deserved a drumroll, but then Ernest and I would be in a *thick* jam. What we saw confused us at first but then became shocking. The man under the mask… was not a *man*.

Ms. Dominus, the assistant principal, sat cross-legged on her "throne." It was shocking, but certainly possible. *Nobody* would doubt the assistant principal of a school being the head of a drug mafia, especially when the principal and superintendent(pretty much his usual, un-illegal bosses) were under her in the chain of command. This was how she was able to afford such an expensive house. It wasn't inherited money; it was illegal money. I realized her good-natured, considerate demeanor was all a cover. She was a wolf in sheep's clothing. Suddenly, Ernest's phone rang loudly, a call from his mom(probably as to what he was doing out of the house at 11 in the night). Everyone turned to look outside. *We were doomed.* We quickly got on our bikes and turned the corner just in the nick of time. "Well, you must know who that is." Ms. Dominus said in her normal tone as she glared at her "loyal" employees. The superintendent spoke up. "We don't know *exactly* who he is, but he goes by the code name SpectersCloak23."

"*SpectersCloak23*," she repeated the name. She thought for a moment, then ordered, "Mrs. Robinson, you hire someone to find out the identity of this perpetrator. Mr. Ayyad, get the legal issues sorted out. We must be ready for a *vital blow.*”

Chapter 27

What's Brewing Underneath

"Abandon the secret chamber and the spiritual life will decay."

- Isaac Watts

Ernest and I were planning to devote one of our training sessions to visiting the DA's factory. Last time, we had only identified DA operations in Portland and Berlin, but we were onto a new lead. We had discovered new messages traced back to Asco, a city close to Livermore. Ernest checked the distance on his phone, and informed me it would take about twenty-eight minutes by bike to get there. So, whatever we did, we needed to make it quick; otherwise, our moms would kill us. When Ernest and I decided on a location, we chose our neighborhood park; we didn't want our parents to think we were going far. I bid farewell to my family, then headed towards the park, my pedaling moving faster than the wind. I parked it on the curbside but didn't see Ernest. As I waited for him to arrive, I sat on one of the green benches overlooking the playground. Our neighborhood park consisted of two parts: the children's park and the big kids' park(of course, these were not the official names, but all the kids referred to them this way). I wasn't a big fan of either park; I had enjoyed the children's park as a kid, then used the area for playdates and meeting neighbors. The children's park had everything at a low height for children to play on, as well as slides with a steep slope and teacup spinners for kids to laugh and play on as they get dizzy. In fact, the rock climbing at that playground was so tiny for me I could stride on it like stairs. It was one of the only times I felt tall. The big kids' playground was for more energetic, athletic people, hence going against my natural, disliking-physical-activity, short sixth-grader self.

It was the only park with swings that being one of the only things there I enjoyed. It also was in a creepy area surrounded by shady trees and a nearby cemetery. The cemetery was a small area of land with granite tombstones of different shapes and sizes. Near them lay bouquets— although I never really ventured there myself, I could smell the faint, sweet fragrance of roses. Many of the stones honored the veterans in our community and other nearby areas. Not many people visited this area, hence leaving anybody who was playing there feeling uneasy or spooked by a sudden blow of wind or an eerie noise in the distance. As a kid, I would have feared horror movies, but now I realize it was a drama created to spark emotion in viewers. A simple marketing technique. There were two large corkscrew climbers in the playground, one situated firmly by itself and one leading to an obstacle course of rope climbing, monkey bars, and slides. The path from the children's playground to the big kids' park was long, depending on the method of transportation. Biking there was dangerous, as the risk of falling was high, and if you fell to your left, you would tumble downhill and end up in the lake. To get there, you would have to start walking on a path adjacent to the large field next to the children's playground. Then, you would continue on the path, which would suddenly make you go downhill, and then up again until you reached the "BEWARE OF SNAKES" sign. Next to the sign, a bridge would be there, which you would have to cross to continue on the path and avoid the residential area(that specific area was full of retired seniors who despised the young generation of troublemakers). After walking uphill for some more time, you will have reached your destination. I was sitting in the children's park, just to avoid extra travel for Ernest. As I sat on the bench, I saw Ms. Dominus, our assistant principal, walking out of a large mansion-like residence. Just knowing that she was the enemy we were trying to fight made me want to go and confront her, but I knew that wouldn't be a smart move.

"Hi, Nathan," Ernest shouted from across the park, his bike parked next to mine. I got up immediately to greet him. We then set on our long journey to Asco, taking smooth streets without any slope. Whew. Today, my legs were in for some real exercise. We hooted and whooped as we speeded across Livermore into Asco, our frail legs having such strength today as they kept pedaling without stopping, the wheel rotating faster and faster. Unfortunately, I hadn't bought a water bottle with me, so after we stopped at our destination, a form of refreshment after the exercise wouldn't be there. Bummer. We had reached the factory Ernest had discovered. But it wasn't what I was expecting. I was expecting a pharmaceutical firm or a drug factory, but what I saw was different. In large, glass letters read:

Stonebrand Labeling

"So this is where the misprints occur. I'll have to consult with Ernest about testing a sample of the Dexeplin pill." I thought as I approached the building for closer inspection. It was quite a large building, something usually found in an urban area. It had two plexiglass doors with company advertisements put behind the glass. As I entered, there was an African-American lady with curly, orange-dyed hair sitting at a reception counter. She was dressed in a gray business suit, her pink polished nails typing quickly, the keyboard producing a "clack" sound. She looked up and saw me, "Welcome to Stonebrand Labeling. Hun, are your parents around?" I was confused as to what to do. I simply shrugged and mumbled, "*They'll be coming soon.*"

She nodded. "Do you know what your parents want labeled? I could ask the team to get a head start." I said, "No, I don't know what they want labeled. I came here by myself." She simply stared, as the both of us were probably finding this conversation very boring. Suddenly, the office phone rang. She picked it up and held it to her ear. "This is the receptionist, Carla Beaufort speaking." I couldn't hear the other end of the line, but she was affirming the statements given by the other person. "Yes, from what I know, the labeling has been finished; the distribution is pending, though. If you'd like, I'll inform the distribution team about the deadline for the payment. Okay, okay, see you later." What did a labeling center have to do with distribution? I mean, sure, labels could be distributed, but she referred to both as two separate things. What *else* was going on in this place? As she paced across the building in her high heels, I stealthily followed her in an attempt to gain information. Dang, this was so fun yet risky. It felt like I was in a spy movie, going on a covert operation to collapse a large illegal business. She opened a door on the right side of the hallway, and as I slid in after her, I realized I had come across the labeling factory. Large machines were designing and pasting labels on items. Well, the *items* other than pill bottles were being labeled in one of the machines in the corner. The main work being done was all on the containers and blister packs of the orange Dexeplin pills. She walked right across the mechanism labor and strolled into an office with a transparent door. As I was about to walk in, she suddenly turned around to see if anyone was watching. I quickly got out of sight, my heart thumping rapidly. *Close one*, I thought. I peeked through the door to see her remove an intricately woven Persian carpet from the ground, exposing a bare wooden floor. She then took out a few loose floorboards, which revealed a small basement door. I was stunned. She glanced around once again to see if anyone was watching, then entered a tunnel and shut the door behind her. I opened the office door, then slowly creaked the door open. I silently shut the door above me as I descended a metal staircase, attempting to make a minimal sound. I tip-toed across the basement floor and then came across a large metal door. A small screen to its right showed different options of how to enter the room. There was a retina scan, thumbprint, and a four-digit number code. The only part I might have been able to crack was the combination lock. I decided to use a simple code where the letter "a" was number one, "b" was number two, and so on. D, the first letter in *Dexeplin*, was four. E was number five. X was the twenty-fourth letter. I entered the code:

4-5-2-4

Surprisingly, I heard a click on the lock, and the keypad said, You have successfully gained access.

Who knew a secretive organization like this could have premises with such easy passwords? I opened the door, and whoa. I had gotten all my answers. When the DA carried out underground operations, that *literally* meant underground operations. Large mechanics different from the ones used on the ground floor were gathering pills, then pouring them into labeled containers and inserting them one by one in packs. Scientists were designing and adding new dosages and thicknesses to the pills and purposely misplacing them in containers with the regular dosage on the label. This was the distribution team. I suddenly noticed something odd happening in one of the vents high on the wall. Two legs popped out, then a torso, then the entire body of a person. It was Ernest, shakily looking down from the ceiling. He saw a vertical pipeline nearby and slid down it, reaching the ground. I waved my hands in the air and signaled for him to come over. He did so, and I whispered, "*I didn't know you had that in you, Ernest. That would require quite some bravery.*" He shrugged. "*I took it from some Among Us inspiration, except I am not the impostor. I arrived late and didn't know where you were, so I tried tracking you from the vents and found you.*" I chuckled, yet careful not to be heard. I saw the front-desk lady tell something to one of the scientists. The scientist gave a brief nod, then headed towards a different part of the factory. I held up my index finger as a gesture for Ernest to wait. The scientist came back, and this time, she returned with Ibby Ayyad. He was dressed in his traditional white robes and turban and walked towards Ms. Beaufort. We shifted to a hiding spot where the conversation was within earshot. “When is the best time to consult with your boss?” he inquired, slightly angered by the event, massaging his beard. “She will be traveling the whole of this week and the week after.” the lady dutifully reported. “Maybe a video conference could work. We still need some more production done before the transaction.” the scientist said. The lady gave Ibby her boss’ contact information and then walked back to resume her normal job. I murmured, “*Is that our cue to go, or shall we continue to hear for more information?*” Ernest’s response was silent, yet louder than a thousand fire alarms. We would stay, of course. They still hadn’t discovered that there were people within the building who weren’t involved in any sort of dirty business. Ibby had begun to use many expletives against Stonebrand Labeling's manager, yet these were words commonly used by most of the middle school population. Ibby did a brief progress check to calculate how much time it would take them to finish production and pay the labeling firm. "Three days," he concluded. "In three days, can we finish the entire production and hand over the cash if we do double the work?" The scientists eyed each other, then replied, "It could be possible, but that would be putting a lot of pressure on us. Then, the multiplying, distribution, and labeling, we might or might not. We'll try our best." Ibby patted the main scientist's shoulder and took a quick look at her nametag. "Dr. Bliant, work can never be done without pressure, and pressure can never be done without work. That's just the way it is. Whatever it is, you *will* do it, or you know what it will cost you. There is and will continue to be no uncertainty on that. *Got it*?" He stared her down, penetrating her emotional defense like a javelin struck right through her shield and armor. She gulped, and her hand quivered. She tilted her head down, regret and shame for what she had said. "And also, you said you would try your best," he announced, now addressing all the pillmakers. "Never try your best. *Do* your best." We decided that this significant moment was the time to leave. We silently waited for Ibby to go back to his office and dismiss the scientists. As the scientists continued to do their work, I signaled for Ernest to come through the door. "*Wait a minute, you broke through THAT door? H-How?*" I gave a sly grin, then tapped my head and pointed it to the sky. He scoffed. "*We shouldn't go through the door because then the lady will have her suspicions on where you went.*" I gave a thumbs-up, and then we shimmied up the pipeline Ernest had previously descended. It was quite difficult, as I wasn't able to get a grip quite well. Ernest was doing it with such expertise; I wondered where he learned the art from. I saw a few objects sticking out of the wall and used my not-so-frequently-used rock climbing skills to make my way into the vent. We then did an army crawl to travel through the narrow, claustrophobic space. Underneath us was a metal part of the vent with small holes in it so we could see each part of the building and navigate our way. When it came to exiting, we came out through a vent near the front desk, unseen by Ms. Beaufort. Now was the hard part. How would we distract Ms. Beaufort to safely get out of the building? Ernest felt around in his pockets. He pulled something out and showed it to me. A smooth, oval-shaped pebble was sitting in his palm, the cream color of the rock blending in with Ernest's skin. "*I'm gonna throw the pebble, then when she's distracted, we move.*" he whispered the command. "*Aye, aye.*" I saluted back. We shared a smile. He hurled it across the room like a baseball pitcher, and it made a noise after coming in contact with the polished marble floor. Ms. Beaufort raised an eyebrow and then went to see what the sound was. We made sure not to make any noise with our feet as we ran to escape the building. Ms. Beaufort looked up, then shook her head and sat in her chair. “Mission accomplished.” I announced. Ernest high-fived me, and we headed towards Livermore in the orange sunset. I sighed as I pedaled my way across Asco. Back to normal, espionage-less life. That was always a good thing. Now, what I needed to do was to eat dinner, practice violin, then sleep. Back and forth from Livermore to Asco was about an hour via bike, so I got a lot of energy exerted today. Hopefully, the physical activity would result in height growth. I can’t stay like this all my life. Not when I had a superpower.

Chapter 28

Can We Get A Taller Firewall?

"Success is not final, failure is not fatal: it is the courage to continue that counts."

– Winston Churchill

Well, after looking at the failures over the past few days, our only hope is that Rey or our once kind and loving assistant principal, Ms. Dominus, doesn't know our identities. It all started after we decoded a message: "We have got a deal. He will be arriving at Palm Shade Beach near Lake del Valle at 6:30." We had visited the site we thought would have caught the criminals red-handed, but no dealing or other such suspicious activities occurred. We would use Ernest's software to disguise our voices and notify the police via phone calls. When the police showed up, they didn't find anyone or anything suspicious going on. We felt guilty and confused as to how we had messed up. It happened once again, this time in Pleasanton. We were sure we had them, that last time was an error of some sort. Yet again, after informing the police and reaching the supposed place again, nothing was found. The failed attempts to catch the culprits weren't the only thing the DA did to try to get us to back off. They had hired a private investigator. He was a tall European man, and I saw him on multiple occasions, but I didn't think he was following me. He communicated in a walkie-talkie, and although I didn't know what he was saying, I was able to intercept the radio frequencies. I asked Ernest to get a sort of "Radio Frequency to Human Language" translation, which I think he called a "receiver." Don't blame me for my obliviousness; I'm not in charge of the tech stuff, *he* is. Ernest converted the frequencies to text, and we read it:

Agent Badaski reporting. I am close to discovering the identity of SpectersCloak23. After further digging through firewall layers, I should be able to find out who the person is. Agent Badaski, over and out.

This was bad news. If our identity was compromised, then we would be in serious trouble, and all the things that could go wrong with a person of my capabilities would proceed. How were we to stop this? "Ernest, can you, like, 'rebuild' the firewall?" I asked desperately. He shrugged. "It's too tedious to do anything with the firewalls, and we don't have that kind of time." We sat in thought, urgently thinking about any possibility of keeping us behind the curtain. "I know!" Ernest shrieked. "I'll need you to deflect the signals he is using to breach our firewall. He is very likely using some sort of platform to create the code to break our protection. All I need you to do is to use your ability to prevent him from gaining access." It was a shame that I didn't even think about what to do with my *own* ability. Ernest certainly was helpful. "That's a great idea." I said, "But how long would I have to keep him waiting? That sounds like a lot of time for both of us." Ernest thought about it. "You could mentally try to flag the results he is using to break through the firewalls as potentially dangerous before it is received, therefore preventing the protection from collapsing and not letting him see our identity. After that, turn off the Internet to make it lag more."

"You came up with that in just a matter of seconds!" I said, awestruck.

He gave me a flaunty grin, just as a "know-it-all" computer whiz would do in this situation. I rolled my eyes.

"Oh, I'm intercepting some frequencies," I said after the weird buzz in my head moved in an erratic pattern of waves.

Agent Badaski reporting. One more security breach is needed before the

identity of SpectersCloak23 is revealed. It will only take a few hours, so I shall complete it and inform you ASAP. After this, I will expect two hundred and fifty dollars to be transferred to my overseas account. I shall inform you of my account details afterward. Agent Badaski, over and out.

We had to act fast. And now. Ernest quickly entered his password to unlock his computer and opened the security application he was using to protect our account. After it showed a warning of a firewall breach in big, red letters, Ernest instructed me to concentrate on the screen and to search for the feeling of passwords and codes going in and out. Ernest had explained to me how this was like a message and that the protection software Ernest had installed received the codes and passwords used to hack into the system in the form of a message. I soon found it after some searching.

Reliable Identity Protection:

(enter- 5ifo330dj30sd) authorization_complete processing-next-query

Mikolaj_Badaski78:

password_bypass_code(source=true?<html dir="ltr" ><head data-info="f:msnallexpusers,prg-sp-liveapi,prg-fic-cpage,infra-ceto 1-t,prg-bd-strc,org-bd-curated-carb,prg-live-stripe2-c,platagyhp3cf,ads-lockerdome**)**

I had never seen a message have such a small font and have never felt that much of a gush of information. The guy was definitely using some hacks to bypass the security info.

Reliable Identity Protection:

(enter- source=true?<html dir="ltr" ><head data-info="f:msnallexpusers,prg-sp-liveapi,prg-fic-cpage,infra-ceto 1-t,prg-bd-strc,org-bd-curated-carb,prg-live-stripe2-c,platagyhp3cf,ads-lockerdome**)**
processing_request authorization_complete firewall_final_secure_page_query

"Ernest, Badaski's about to hack!" I exclaimed with fear. Ernest replied calmly, "Nathan, all you gotta do is reroute the message to a place where it won't be retrieved, and the protection software will analyze the request as invalid." I let out a deep breath and concentrated on any message by the agent I'd need to disrupt.

Mikolaj_Badaski78:

firewall_bypass_code(gen-password_code)<html dir="ltr" ><head data-info="f:msnallexp1users,prg-sp-livea&pi,prg-fic-cpage,infra-ceto 1-t,prg-bd-strc,org-bd-curated-carb,prg-live-str3ipe2-c,platagyhp4cf,ads-lockerdome

Password_derived:?Titanium22#!^*

Concentrating on the digital information, I mentally pretended it was a cart of books from the library, and I needed to push that cart as fast as I could to Mrs. Cabrera's room. I pushed with such force, so much energy wasted just in getting those English to Spanish dictionaries and thesauri to the room. And finally, I did.

Reliable Identity Protection:

(enter-
?Titanium22#!^*)
processing_request
authorization_incomplete
result:invalid_information
blocking-
(Mikolaj_Badaski78)
username_restricted

"Agent Badaski has been officially blocked." I declared victoriously to Ernest, who patiently awaited my inner message battle to end. He said, "See, I knew you could do it." He wasn't as impressed or surprised as I had hoped for him to be. Well, that was what coaches were like. They were rarely impressed with their students, but when the coaches *were* impressed, the students would be overjoyed with themselves. Even though Ernest didn't have my power, I knew he could have controlled it and discovered all his abilities *way* faster than I had. Or maybe not, and I was just underestimating myself. "Well, I should get going," I said, rising from a seat in the janitors' room, relieved to escape from the strong scent of bleach and cleaning fluids. "Oh, and thank you, Ernest. I wouldn't have been able to stop the agent without your advice." I thanked him. Ernest patted me on the shoulder. "Friends always have each others' backs," he said, trying to imply that my gratitude wasn't necessary. I lifted my backpack and wore it, then seated myself on my bike. I saluted Ernest to say goodbye, and I rode back to my house.

Chapter 29

Failed Attempts at Justice

"Justice itself tends to be corrupted by political passion."

– T. S. Eliot

The last time we tried to catch the DA, we ended up failing. But this time, we would take all the information Ernest and I had collected. Documents, photographs, articles, although we couldn't share my messages, which was probably the main source of our information. We would notify the police by piecing together newspaper cut-outs to make words on a page, like the ransom notes in detective shows. After an hour of cutting out letters from newspapers and magazines, we produced a note:

Hi,

HeRe ArE some docments, photographs, and miscellaneous evidence against the Dexeplin Association. Please look through.

After pasting the letters, we folded the letter and sealed it in an envelope, cautiously avoiding any fingerprints or any of our other DNA materials to come on the note. When we sealed the envelope, we used tape instead of saliva(I wouldn't have used spit anyway, for sanitary purposes). Now, the job was simple; I was a little boy, and somebody asked me to mail this to the police station. I was too scared to go in, so I would kindly ask somebody on the street to drop it off for me. We carried out the plan. After riding towards the local station, we parked near the street corner. I found a red-haired lady in a floral dress carrying a small purple handbag. I innocently said, "Ma'am, somebody asked me to give this to the police, and I'm too scared to go in. Would you mind if I asked you to do so *for me*?" I added the last two words with a naïve, convincing tone. She gave me an affectionate smile and said, "Sure, sweetheart, I'll do it for you." I watched from the same place as she walked over to the police station and handed this letter to an officer nearby. I couldn't hear what she was saying, but I could make out the words "kid on the street" and "asked me to give." The officer gestured for her to enter the station. I waited for quite some time, but they didn't seem to be coming out. It was a good thirty minutes before a government van pulled up, and three officers and a man in a black suit stepped out. The lady I asked to go to the station had heavy, metal handcuffs on her delicate hands, and she was forcefully put in the van. The van screeched as it made a large U-turn and proceeded off into the distance. *Oh, fish*. I had made a grave blunder.

I needed to find a way to save that lady and break the DA. Ernest and I both regretted the decision of involving an innocent, oblivious Samaritan. Ernest asked me if I managed to pick up the car plate number, their phone number, or their IMEI number, at least. I told him that I was able to get the phone number and IMEI number of the agents in the car, as well as the lady. Ernest was relieved. After training with Ernest for a long time, I not only increased my span of interception, but I can now trace the IMEI number as well. An IMEI number is a fifteen-digit number unique to each cellphone and is useful in tracking devices without SIM cards. “Now it will be easy to track their location.” Ernest always had a Plan B in his belt; we rescue the woman and find a better way to get this evidence to an official, probably high up in the ranks and not corrupt. We carried that out the next day. Ernest had the location of the lady’s phone since the other officers were out doing their duty. There was still one officer with her, though. *Just for surveillance*, I guessed. We followed Ernest’s directions until we reached the red pinpoints on his phone. We ended up in front of an abandoned warehouse on the border of Livermore and Asco, the city where Stonebrand Labeling was. Ernest whispered, "*We've done these stealth missions before, so I don't think it'll be a problem. I go in, take a glance at the area, and come out. I'll get an idea of what we have to do.*" I nodded, and he creaked open the door. He swiftly slid through the thin space and faded into the darkness to explore. I patiently awaited his arrival, and within five minutes, he returned. He panted, "*There are fire alarms. They are connected to the fire sprinkler system. That will be a pretty good distraction. There is also an ax for breaking glass in case of an emergency. We'll use that to free her.*"

I was amazed at how Ernest thought of solutions based on the resources given. That was a really good skill to have. Maybe his life wouldn't be limited to software, programming, or computer engineering. For all I knew, he would be pretty good in the military, too. "*And one thing,*" he said right before we would execute the plan. "*It's too risky to bring her along with us. She can escape herself.*" Before I broke out into protest, I considered what he said. It would be inconvenient for us to take her along with us. What if we got caught? I reached out my hand, and he shook it to show our agreement. "*Let's start this rescue mission,*" I said energetically. We slid through the door, and I followed Ernest as we sneaked across rooms and found a fire alarm. We pushed the switch in and pulled it down. A loud blaring sound was heard, and small sprinkler heads popped out of the ceiling, spraying water in each direction. Ernest found a large brick on the ground and threw it at the glass covering the ax. We were careful not to step on the shattered shards, and I grabbed the ax. We still could have used the glass to break open the rope tying the woman, but it would look cooler and would have been more efficient to use an ax. I didn't want to free the lady because my safety was important. It wasn't like I wanted to put Ernest in danger, but at least the lady would be in confusion. I handed the ax to Ernest, and he cut through the rope in one smooth action. He removed the bag over her face and covered his own. He pointed towards the emergency "exit," and she headed in that direction. After she left, we ran out the way we came. We continued to watch inside and saw an officer run in his drenched uniform, and he muttered something angrily into his walkie-talkie. This was our cue to leave. We got on our bikes, wore our helmets, and took off. Now wasn't the time to celebrate our victory. Heck, we can't even *celebrate* any victory. We still had a lot to do. Ernest and I parted ways at a fork in the road so we could go to our homes. At home, as I helped my mom prepare dinner, I was going to ask about any police officers we knew. I would explain the purpose of the question like this, "We are making a thank-you note in school to the people in law enforcement." As we ate the delicious tacos my mom had prepared,

I asked and explained myself. Actually, *now* I was kind of going back on my decision because I remembered that Ibby was my dad's friend, but he turned out to be a villain. Could I really rely on my parents' contacts? "Sofie, don't you know Officer Trovare?" my dad asked, mouth half-full. "Oh yeah," my mom said. "Noemi's ballet teacher." I was puzzled. "Um, I think I asked for a *police* officer, not a ballet teacher."

"Nathan the Nincompoop, haven't we mentioned this before? Mrs. Trovare does ballet as a side job and mainly works in the police. She used to work as a case manager in MedWatch." Noemi said without looking. I was thoroughly roasted by my sister because of my unaware and careless attitude towards her personal life. "Who uses *nincompoop* nowadays?" I asked, just to get back at her.

"There couldn't have been a better word to describe you. Your stupidity resurfaced a *dead word*."

I had to shut up now.

"Well, I can tell you, Nathan, she is probably the only officer we know." my dad concluded. "Does she live nearby?" I asked. "No, she lives down in Albuquerque." I sighed and rubbed my thumb against my fingers to get the crumbs off. Now, what would I say? It would seem unusual to ask my parents to talk to this woman. I'd have to find a way to see her character and see if she was trustworthy or not. That night, I sneaked into my parents' room to check my mom's contacts. I found "Officer Trovare" saved in my mom's phone. The only messages between the two were related to the scheduling of Noemi's classes. I viewed her profile picture, which proudly displayed her golden badge honoring the Albuquerque police. I looked at her number, saved it in my head, and wrote it down later so I wouldn't forget. I would show Ernest tomorrow, and we would figure something out. Hopefully.

At Ernest's place, I showed him the number I had written down. We thought about what to do and quickly formulated a plan. We would text that number using an anonymous account and then lure her in by telling her that they had important intelligence regarding a case. Then, we would ask her to join a Google Meet. This was quite risky, but Ernest said he would prevent location trackers, put a voice modifier, and ensure safety. We wouldn't turn on our camera. Ernest created the profile and saved the contact name as "Doogle Gocks." He now contacted Officer Trovare's number, and I got the message:

+(925)-346-XXXX:

Hello, Officer. I have some significant information involving a case. Care to join this meeting? meet.google.com/myc-cpga-omf

After a few moments, we received a response.

+(505)-945-XXXX:

I have joined your meeting. I am expecting some profuse intel.

We joined our meeting and found a lady with a ponytail sitting back on her chair. She was sitting in a room with a large bulletin board about a case, a thread linking details to each other. She started the conversation. “Hello, Mr. Gocks, please make this quick. I have other matters to attend to.” We laughed at the seriousness she displayed when she said, “Mr. Gocks.” Ernest installed a voice modifier and then spoke. “Officer Trovare, have you heard about the Dexeplin Association?” She scrunched up her nose and then replied, “Yes. The company that makes focus medications for children. What about it?” We cautiously said the next few words, “We have sent you major pieces of evidence that show clear fraudulence. They have increased the potency of the pill illegally, resulting in many children having gotten addicted and *died* because of these pills." I recalled Morty's candlelight vigil. She quickly looked through the proof we sent to her phone, and her eyes widened after each swipe. I knew this would definitely be in her interests, given her work history. "Okay, but what do you want *me* to do with this? This is more for the drug authorities, FBI, or other higher officials. An officer in my position won't do you much good. I could have done something earlier, but now I won't have the same impact. I'm just loyal to the government and will work my way up with that."

"Exactly," Ernest replied to her self-doubt. "We tried bringing this to the attention of the police before, but they were all too corrupt to do anything about it. We met a dutiful officer like you, and we rely on you to fix this." She thought about it for a second, a pen clicking in her hand. "Okay, you haven't provided me with any locations yet, so once you have done that, I'll bring my team with me to the spot. We'll raid the area, arrest those involved, and prove them guilty in court with your evidence." She brilliantly laid out the series of events without us having to do it. "Thank you," Ernest said. "It's always my pleasure to do what's right," she replied. We exited the meeting. We had found the right person for the job.

After sending the DA's locations, we awaited a message from Officer Trovare. We didn't know if she would tell us when she planned to storm the DA's base, catch them by surprise, and send them to jail. We anticipated it, and our prediction was right. She was just probably curious to see who we were.

+(505)-945-XXXX:

My team and I are on our way to the airport. We received a search warrant and permission from the narcotics bureau. We'll fly into Livermore, spend the night, and execute the plan tomorrow morning.

+(925)-346-XXXX:

[U+1F44D]

Ernest had sent a thumbs-up emoji to her.

+(505)-945-XXXX:

Also, how did you get my contact? This question makes me think we know each other.

I gulped. We had to think of something. What if she found out who we were? Actually, that was the wrong question. I got the contact info from my mom. I just *hoped* my family wouldn't get dragged into this mess.

+(925)-346-XXXX:

We are vigilantes. This time, we wanted to solve a crime with the help of the law. We found you with our advanced database and figured you would be the right one.

Thank you,

Mr. Gocks & Mr. Specter

At least the conversation was resolved, but now she would be confused as to who “Mr. Specter” was. She didn’t reply, but now she knew a little more. She would think it was a team of two now, but our identities still weren’t exposed. I could barely sleep that night. Was it really this easy? What if something went sideways? What if the Dexeplin Association didn’t collapse? These questions rang in my ears all night. Since I tried for an hour or two and didn’t sleep a wink, I went to my bedroom bookshelf and pulled out *A is for Alibi* by Sue Grafon. I stopped at page 152 at 1:33 and closed my eyes.

Chapter 30

Raid and Arrest

"In the end, crime doesn't pay."

– Lane Garrison

I chugged my *chai* and stuffed some snacks into my mouth as I was in a hurry to leave. I needed to get there on time so we could go back to Stonebrand. "Eat a little more and go; what's the hurry?" My mom called after me. "Gotta go, bye!" I managed to say with food in my mouth. My mom shook her head. "*These teens*," my mom said under her breath. "*And my son isn't even one yet!*" I could understand her frustration, but today was quite important. I don't think I would rush any meetings with Ernest after this one, so this was one exception. I pedaled faster than a cheetah and gasped when I found Ernest waiting for me in the neighborhood park. "A little late," he smirked. “Sorry, Mom was forcing me to eat a little more snacks.” I defended myself. We proceeded to reach Asco and found ourselves passing the warehouse we rescued that lady from. We parked at a dentist’s clinic next door to the labeling factory. I suddenly remembered something. “Ernest, do you have your phone on you?” I asked with a slight urgency. “Always do,” he said and pulled it out of his shirt pocket. “Text the officer and inform her of the secret room,” I said. She was a detective, after all. I didn’t doubt her skills. But in case she missed the secret room, we had to inform her.

+(925)-346-XXXX:

There is a secret room located under the carpet in the office behind the labeling. That is where you will find the production center.

+(525)-945-XXXX:

Wow. I thought secret rooms only happened in the movies. Thanks.

Moments later, two police vans pulled up in front of Stonebrand Labeling. Officer Trovare, two policemen, and a policewoman kicked open the door of their vehicles, raised their guns, and broke open the doors of the building with such force I was afraid the building would come down. *Dang*, and I thought ballerinas were delicate. We tip-toed to Stonebrand for a closer look. “HANDS UP!” they commanded Ms. Beaufort as she fearfully escorted them to the secret room. This was it! We entered the building then entered a vent. We crawled our way to the vent above the secret room to see what was going on. We saw one of Trovare’s men taking photos of the room and the pills. Several scientists were in handcuffs, including Mr. Ayyad. Suddenly, a door swung open, and the Livermore police force stormed in. Ms. Dominus paced coolly after the chaotic entry. “Albuquerque Police,” yelled a blond policeman on Ibby’s side. “Why are you doing this search and seizure? You got a warrant?” Officer Trovare lifted up a folded paper from her pocket. “I have evidence to back me up, too, and it involves a case of falsified ingredient reporting.” The policeman sighed. He said to Ms. Dominus, “Sorry, ma’am. They’ve got evidence and a warrant.” Ms. Dominus had a look of disappointment and shock as to how her forces had abandoned her so easily. She shook her head, dissatisfied. “*Nathan, Ernest…*” she called out innocently, searching for us around the factory. We ducked out of view from the vent, even though it would be unlikely she spotted us. Still, a criminal mastermind would be pretty attentive. “It was foolish of me. All this time, searching in school, a Mister X who fought for student justice, then stuck his nose in my business. I never, in my wildest dreams, could think it was *you two*.” She suddenly looked up, her eyes focused on the vent. I held my breath. She paced around once again.

"I was mindless to have let the search for your identity go at that time. I thought that there wouldn't be any problem, that *you* wouldn't be a problem. But then you stuck like a weed, secretly obstructing my progress. Your silly attempts at bringing justice, peace, and all that hogwash to society began to grow. And it very negatively affected me." She sucked in a deep breath of frustration. "You know, success is all that matters to me. The Dexeplin Association would guarantee me that. Who would care if a few students died here and there? It is simply the students' success and *my* success that matters to me. So, I created the company and hired many under the guise of Rey Ronaldo. And so everyone thought I was a man!" She cackled sinisterly. "Bloody masculine-minded society. Good thing I did choir in my school days. Voice manipulation served me well. Anyways, I'm tired of playing hide-and-seek." She pulled out a revolver from her pocket and aimed at the police. It was my time to act. While the officers were coaxing her to put her gun down and raise her hands, I focused all my mind and energy on Ms. Dominus' phone. Soon enough, her cell phone burst and ignited in her pocket, and she cried out in pain and surprise. She fired in all directions, and the police had to duck to save their skin. Many production machines were hit, and sparks and smoke emerged. Soon, when she had no bullets left, the police extinguished the flames. Officer Trovare pinned Ms. Dominus to the wall and cuffed her. The officer blew hair out of her face and wiped her sweat with the back of her hand. "And a grand finale," she said sarcastically. We went back to the entrance vent and got out of the place just after they left. We didn't want to suffer from claustrophobia. We saw the police gently put the criminals' heads into their vans when they had so forcefully invaded and cuffed them. It certainly was ironic. The police vans headed on their way, and Ernest and I fist-bumped and high-fived each other. Our definition of celebration wasn't that extravagant. We were beyond satisfied on the inside, though.

Morty's truth would finally be recognized, and his death wouldn't be shrugged off or forgotten. I had avenged him. Not to sound like a bloodthirsty warlord, but the reason Morty passed would be a lesson to all. Ernest pulled out his phone to thank the officers.

+(925)-346-XXXX:

Thank you for helping us. We greatly appreciate your support.

+(505)-945-XXXX:

As I said, it is always my pleasure. We will send them to the Livermore police station and hand over the evidence. We shall stay for a few more days to testify in court.

As we biked back home, we felt a huge burden lifted off of our shoulders, like we were escaping what we did. Should we have continued to do this, or were we over with all the "solving crimes" stuff? Would this be the *last* time Ernest and I spent time together? I told myself not to ponder such thoughts. Such feats weren't easy, and I needed to chill. Take a break. Which sixth grader stops crimes in his school, proceeds to stop a large pharma company from overdosing kids, and goes to school at the same time? But I was forgetting one thing. This ordeal wasn't over. We had to get it proved in court. Only then would people learn the lesson we wanted to pass. But that could wait. Now, I just needed to spend time at home, celebrating(without revealing anything) with my family.

Epilogue

"There will come a time when you believe everything is finished. That will be the beginning."
– Louis L'Amour

ONE YEAR LATER
MARCH 16, 2020

Well, conflicts always happen. They are *bound* to keep coming into our lives. I have learned that in my life. It was a Monday, yet I wasn't going to school. The norms were broken. Instead, I was to blankly stare at my 7th grade English teacher through the computer as she poorly organized the online learning. It was one of the only times I wore my glasses for this long of a duration. Everything was closed, and nobody dared to go outside due to the lockdown. COVID-19, a dangerous virus, had spread all over the world, and now we had to get used to remote learning. This was all new, and I didn't know if this meant the messages would increase or not. I had gotten pretty used to them, and my mind was more stable with them compared to when I started.

The Dexeplin Association's case was resolved in court, and the evidence we had, along with the police's help, let Erica Dominus alias Rey Ronaldo, Kelly Robinson, Lloyd Davenport, and many others involved in the increased potency and mislabeling of the Dexeplin pills (although it seemed like Ibby fled the country or something, because the police weren't able to find a trace of him. That did increase the amount of wanted posters he had). Morty's demise and the arrests had finally given people the concern to make sure what they were giving their kids was safe. Ever since my dad found out that Ibby was involved in this crime, he has referred to him with all the Hindi cuss words. It's good to add to my internal Hindi dictionary. My mom has scolded him many times for using bad language in front of Noemi and me, but we didn't mind.

Mrs. Trovare had written a book called *Mr. Gocks and Mr. Specter: The Online Policemen*. She obviously didn't make it "based on true events." She simply called it a "figment of her imagination" and wrote about how we brought crimes to the police's attention. The book's cover had a silhouette of two men with a hat and glasses. The regular depiction of hackers. I had read her book and found many similarities to the way we informed her about the DA. The book wasn't that big of a hit, as her writing skills weren't exceptional. They were… *okay*, I supposed. I was very judgemental when it came to books, as I had read so many.

I was catching some messages from Google Hangouts. The teachers told us to use it for contacting teachers or friends if they had any questions.

Luke Robinson:

Hey, Nathan.

I wasn't expecting Luke, the troublemaker from Reagan Middle School, to contact me.

Luke Robinson:

Remember me? Ever since we met, I always knew there was some odd connection between us.

This was starting to get creepy. I felt uneasy.

Luke Robinson:

Turns out, I found out exactly what. You have what I have, Nathan. We both can read minds and gauge people's secrets.

Oh, *no*. It couldn't be. Why did God have to choose the *most wrong* person to have my power? Was he just blabbering? He couldn't have it, no. But if he did, then my safety was at risk.

Luke Robinson:

I wish we could be friends. We would have been so powerful together. But putting my mom in jail that's something I'll never forgive you for. So, congrats on being my new enemy.

I took a look at Luke's last name. Oh. Kelly Robinson, superintendent of Livermore Unified School District, was his mom. I was in deep fecal matter. There was no better way to describe my dire situation.

Luke Robinson:

I'll see you on the battlefield.[U+2694]

I generally wasn't the type for war. But I still could sharpen my defense. And this wasn't a polite request. It was a challenge. A challenge I was willing to face. If I was in danger due to an enemy with my power, I needed to protect myself and the people I love. So, let the war begin!

Ms. Dominus, her once colorful clothes now a tight orange uniform, was terribly angered and mentally affected by her imprisonment. She had never even considered that she would even have a trial, much less going to jail. She had been told by an officer that a man by the name of Mayih Byraadi was here to see her. Although at first she thought it was some reporter or journalist here to write about her, it suddenly hit her who it was. A man with a clean-shaven head and mask entered. He wore an Adidas sweater and jeans, but it was unmistakably him. Ms. Dominus picked up the phone to speak. “Hello, Mr. Ayyad. Your clever anagram and new look would fool most,” she said scornfully. “*Thank you, I guess? You know I’m not supposed to be here,*” he said under his teeth. “*What’s our next plan of action? Are we done forever?*” She took a deep breath and organized her thoughts methodically. “I’m gonna be really honest with you. The DA is dead, period. But to avenge the fall of our drug empire, it is quite simple. Find Nathan Bauer. I hear you’re quite well associated with his family." He blinked at her and cleared his throat. "*Nathan Bauer? Short sixth-grade kid with black hair and sea-green eyes?*" She nodded. He was terribly confused. She proceeded to explain who was looking to destroy the Dexeplin Association, who secretly got evidence, took information from the superintendent, and how she found out. He stared at her, wide-eyed in disbelief. "*But the lockdown will prevent anything from happening.*" She shrugged playfully, "I don't know how you're going to do it, but if you successfully carry out the mission, you will be rewarded the sum of one million dollars." His eyes widened. Clearly, greed was the trick. "*Okay, I'll try. Right now, I'm in danger of getting caught, so I am about to board a plane to Casablanca. During this time, I shall plan out the execution of the task and hire people.*" Ms. Dominus showed Ibby her ring, then curled her hand into a fist. Ibby did the same to show loyalty to the fallen DA.

TO BE CONTINUED...

Afterword

The nerves in our brain are like a complicated system of wires, all connected by synapses. Now, a phone's internal structure is very complex as well, involving similar connections between functions. When you send a message to someone, radio waves with a particular frequency are sent to a nearby cell tower or satellite, which then transfers the information to the nearest cell tower to the recipient. After I joined these ideas, *3G: Nathan* was born. I imagined him as a kid with a 21st-century superpower. Who knows, maybe in the distant future, science will evolve to an extent where this is possible. Our fingers won't be used to control our devices then; our minds will do it all. As Nathan showed us in this book, crime prevention will become easier and use less effort. He went through dangerous adventures and put criminals where they belonged, all with the help of his message interception.

I certainly hope you enjoyed this book and were engaged in Nathan's journey throughout the story.

Saai

www.ingramcontent.com/pod-product-compliance
Ingram Content Group UK Ltd
Pitfield, Milton Keynes, MK11 3LW, UK
UKHW062253290726
14090UKWH00017B/671